NIFTY
FIFTY

50 CRYPTIC CROSSWORDS
WITH AN AUSSIE FLAVOUR

Clan Destine
PRESS

by WILLSIN ROWE & FIN J ROSS

First published by Clan Destine Press in 2020
Clan Destine Press
PO Box 121, Bittern
Victoria 3918 Australia

National Library of Australia Cataloguing-In-Publication data:
Rowe, Willsin & Ross, Fin J.
Nifty Fifty; 50 Cryptic Crosswords with an Aussie Flavour
ISBN: 978-0-6450021-1-9 (pb)

Cover Design, Design & Typesetting: Willsin Rowe

www.clandestinepress.net

INTRODUCTION

Welcome to the world of cryptic crosswords. For the uninitiated, cryptic crosswords appear to be just as they are intended; mystifying, illogical, perplexing and downright frustrating.

While it's true that most clues don't appear to make much sense, they should actually read logically. Sometimes the answers are literally staring you in the face; it's just that the untrained eye can't see them. Sometimes they're obscured by traps designed to throw you off the track. But start thinking a bit laterally and the fog will begin to lift and the nonsensical will start to make perfect sense.

There's really only three prerequisites to being able to solve cryptic crosswords. Firstly, you really DO need to be able to spell or you'll have a nightmare trying to unravel anagrams. Secondly, you have to be able to think laterally and have a real appreciation for words and their many different nuances of meaning. Thirdly, you really need to be a bit warped or twisted.

One of the first things to do when looking at a cryptic crossword is to put aside the usual way you might read or interpret a sentence. What you are actually trying to do is crack a code. When learning the basics of solving cryptic clues, it should be noted however, that while most compilers follow certain, universal rules, each employs his or her own bag of tricks which may bend those rules somewhat. Just remember that no two setters will necessarily adhere to the same code.

Given that **The Nifty Fifty** are compiled by two different setters—one male, one female—the style of clues may vary.

The basic principle of a cryptic clue is that it should always (well almost always) have two means of arriving at the answer—a straight definition and a roundabout or 'cryptic' means of finding the word. Sometimes, however, on first reading a clue, it is not immediately obvious which word is the 'key' or 'definition' word, but it's most commonly the first or last word of the clue.

ANAGRAMS

These are probably the most useful tool for cryptic compilers. Generally speaking, if an anagram is involved there will be a key word—called an 'anagrind'—to indicate that the word or words immediately before or after it form an anagram. Anagrinds can be simple words like 'about', 'new', 'perhaps', 'twisted' or 'scrambled' or they can be very cleverly devised to aid the sense—or 'surface' reading of the clue.

For example: Experts unravelled case (4)

Here, 'unravelled' is the anagrind, indicating that the four-letter answer is an anagram of 'case' – ie. ACES.

Laze, to outrage of enthusiast (6)

Here, 'outrage' is the anagrind, indicating an anagram of 'Laze, to' – ie. ZEALOT.

LETTER INDICATORS

An anagram may not necessarily form the whole answer, but may appear in conjunction with another device such as a single letter to achieve the required number of letters. Often, a whole word in a clue will be the means of supplying a single letter or maybe two in the answer.

The list of single letter indicators is vast and requires the solver to have a good knowledge of abbreviations, compass bearings, Roman numerals, chemical symbols and States (both Australian and U.S.) and dozens more.

For example: Note foreign lingo about leering (6)

In this instance 'note' is the musical note 'G'. 'Foreign' is an anagram indicator directing you to use the letters of 'lingo', 'about' tells you that the anagram letters enclose the letter G. Leering is the definition so you're looking for another word for leering; in this case, OGLING.

The letters N, S, E or W may be indicated by Point, Bearing, Quarter or Direction.

Roman numerals are commonly used and may be indicated by the use of the word "Roman" or merely as number, small number, large number etc.

For example: four Romans in a clue indicate that the letters IV appear somewhere together in the answer. Look for the use of V, VI, X, L, C, D or M. A single roman is I.

Love, nothing, duck or ring can mean O.

State can indicate V or VIC, WA, SA, TAS or US state abbreviations such as PA (Pennsylvania), VA (Virginia) or LA (Louisiana).

Note or Key usually indicates musical notes ie A, B, C, D, E, F, G or Do Re Mi etc.

Other musical terms are often applied; for instance, *loud* or *noisy* give you F (forte), *very loud* gives you FF, while *soft* or *quiet* give you P (piano) or *very soft* PP (pianissimo).

Chemical symbols are handy to know, too; ie Potassium (K), Gold (AU) or Silver (AG) etc. Careful though because gold could also be OR (French).

If you see Queen, Her Majesty or maybe ruler or monarch in a clue it invariably leads you to ER; ie Elizabeth Regina. Princess commonly give you 'Di'.

A few other tips:
- While, During, Because, Like = AS
- Church, Child, Award, Honour can be CH
- Party or Function = DO
- Former, Old Girlfriend/Wife/Husband and Once = EX
- Ship, Vessel or Steamer = SS

HOMONYMS

When homonyms are used, they are usually indicated by a key word such as hear, heard, they say, told, in speech etc. Some single letters can be indicated by homonyms.

For example: 'why' = Y; 'sea' or 'see' = C; 'ease' = EE; 'tea' or 'tee' = T; 'be' or 'bee' = B; 'eye' = I.

Homonyms can be used in several ways, for example a clue might give you a synonym for a word but require another word which is spelt differently but sounds the same.

For example: Carry, I hear, naked (4) …could be 'bear' or 'bare'.

HIDDEN WORDS

Sometimes the answer is literally staring you in the face but might be buried within a word or words or may even appear backwards in the clue. Generally, the use of a key word such as inside, embraces, swallows, holds, captures or features may indicate this.

For example: Otto talked partly for a score (5) = TOTAL

These aren't always as easy to spot as you may think. Some compilers deliberately make their clues long enough so that the word may run from one line to the next.

PUNCTUATION

One of the basic principles of cryptics is to ignore all punctuation in a clue. Seldom is it there to help you. More likely it is there to throw you off the track.

Watch particularly commas, question marks and hyphens as they can dramatically alter how a clue is read. Full stops also can be thrown in quite unnecessarily to make you think that one word has no connection to the next.

For example: Horse call-out note is near (4)

In this instance what you really need to read is Horse-call, out note, is near. This gives you neigh for a horse call and out note tells you to drop the E, giving you 'nigh', a synonym for near.

ENCLOSED WORDS

Sometimes, to arrive at an answer you are directed, however vaguely, to put a word or letters inside or outside another word or letters. Pointers here might be: in, inside, enclosed or within or outside, around, from, embracing or surrounding.

For example: Candle fat for everyone, love, in Tweed Heads (6)

Here, 'everyone' = 'all', 'love' = 'O' inside TW (from Tweed) = TALLOW (candle fat)

FIRST and LAST

Single or groups of letters can be indicated by the use of indicator words such as:

Initial, first, prime, capital or leading. These words are usually directing you to take the first letter of the word either immediately preceding or after the key word. Just remember it may be used in an everyday context to throw you off the track.

> *For example:* Leading lady gives you L.

Watch out though for words like Skinhead or Clifftop which would give you S and C respectively. If these words are pluralised or written as first two for example it's telling you to use the first two letters of the next or previous word. The same rule applies to the last letters of words which may be indicated by words such as final, ultimate, last or end. For example: Final countdown gives you N.

DELETING LETTERS:

Sometimes letters need to be deleted from the words in a clue, just as they can be added.

Some key words to indicate deletion are headless, decapitated, endless, bottomless, off, out, go, truncated, docked etc.

DOUBLE MEANINGS

Never automatically take a word at face value as many have double meanings; some more obvious than others.

> *For example:* Flower may mean the obvious…or it might be
> something that flows, such as a river.

Runner may mean an athlete or could also be a river, or even a bean.

Number could be a digit or Roman numeral or it could be an anaesthetic (something that numbs) such as ether.

Turner could be a lathe worker, a wheel or screw or even the artist.

FOREIGN WORDS

Simple foreign words (usually European) often appear in cryptics, so a basic knowledge of some French, German, Italian and Spanish pronouns is very handy. Generally, foreign words will be identified by key words such as foreign, French, Parisian, German, Abroad, Overseas, European etc.

> Examples include: The Parisian could be LE or LA ("the" in French) or possibly IL or ELLE (he or she).
>
> A French, or French one may be UN or UNE.
>
> The German will be DER.
>
> The Spanish will be EL.

ODDS and EVENS

The word 'odd' is a useful one for crossword compilers because it has more than one use. It can be used to indicate an anagram but it can also direct you to use only the 'odd', that is the first, third, fifth (etc) letters in the following or preceding words to find the answer.

Similarly, 'even' can direct you to use every second letter to have an answer emerge.

PUZZLERS... START YOUR ENGINES!

PUZZLE #1

ACROSS
1. Basil is one in fixed fizzy powder (7)
5. Blind diggers eat bismuth for decorative hangers (7)
9. Joy whirls, spins heap (9)
10. Texas mission in the heart of gala month (5)
11. Nobleman puts potassium on damaged thing (6)
12. Enclosure holds exaggerated cabin (7)
14. Nothing has one in fastener (4)
15. From now on, chicken church is in favour of their horned heads (10)
19. Five inch policeman, evict chaos with revenge aforethought (10)
20. Russian agrees to four within celebrated singer (4)
22. Entertained royal every day, initially (7)
25. Provide right measure for returning Communist (6)
27. Architectural order found in patio niche (5)
28. Cool cheat blurs dark treat (9)
29. Leer oddly after headless body breaks alpine vocalist (7)
30. Important way foreigner invades (7)

DOWN
1. Oh so funny in central London (4)
2. Former cookware charged atom with growth (9)
3. Link wife with good heart (6)
4. I hear you meet Trent Spooner for therapy (9)
5. Total returns chip for a song (5)
6. Best friends' heads surround busted floats for launch (5,3)
7. One shopping centre returns to Andean animal (5)
8. 10p coin, tails down, will do this bathroom sprayer (6,4)
13. Institution where unit is very confused (10)
16. Yawning spelunker refuses America (9)
17. I say again: I tear tree around (9)
18. Large scale food guard at fifty-one Celcius has calm centre (9)
21. Broken loner left to sign up (6)
23. Sodium in deity produces gametes (5)
24. Shortened month with alternative colour scheme (5)
26. Gave temporarily to allow north in (4)

PUZZLE #2

ACROSS

1. Maul alien terribly, but wear it to keep safe (5)
5. See 21 across
9. Gnu leant awkwardly to straighten out (8)
10. Can, after attempt to render blubber oil (6)
11. Nag added clause to define sportsman (10)
13. Workers Stan wriggled around to find (4)
14. Jigsaw and lathe cut out this stick (4)
15. Cleaner reacts badly to letters from funny individuals (10)
18. Behind us, tan I had held language (10)
20. Unexpected gifts lose the top fruit (4)
21. & 5ac. Quiet fiancé Fisk redirected North was sanctimonious according to Dickens (4,8)
23. Acid returns in file to get through (10)
25. Aged have knowledge about blonde (6)
26. Oils rage about in the harem (8)
28. Slaughterhouse worried less about hamburger presser being out (8)
29. Next to see bid torn apart (6)

DOWN

2. Composer rewrote "Am not Ivan the Terrible" (9)
3. Foolishly said lie was connected (7)
4. Fight against carrying label (3)
5. Very quietly outstepped the horse (5)
6. Lacier train trips involving different tribes (11)
7. What birds do when overtaking to see it at an airshow (3,4)
8. Float about in the air (5)
12. Hymn relating to a withdrawal (11)
16. Alias Shaka Zulu may have had (1,1,1)
17. Correct, watch after. If you're in it, you're sane (5,4)
19. Doe mucked about shed. Many point to realm of peers (7)
20. Seeks food a long time (7)
22. Ina left China after tumultuous eon to seek someone older than Meethuselah (5)
24. Joins together to employ in 20 ends (5)
27. Bone-hunting tribe loses the top point (3)

#2

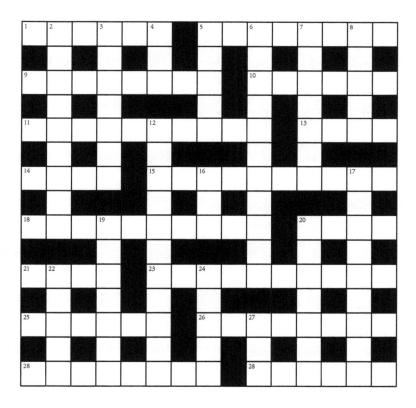

PUZZLE #3

ACROSS

1. Post office in street-car route will rebound (10)
6. Initially, some want sailor to clean deck (4)
10. Tilt angry beagle on the outside (5)
11. The second year to soak my house around Oregon (9)
12. Give over a portion, good-looking (8)
13. Climb like Penny (6)
15. Speedy parking amid invasion (5)
17. Born with sweet head, eats in poverty (9)
18. Reptile oddly as lilting last worry (9)
20. Growth plate after many (5)
22. Outclasses model posteriors (6)
23. Cat spilled one tub east to energise (8)
26. Tiny dog at church returns greeting, beginning under amateur hymns—usually awful (9)
27. At first, cash rate extends past European pancake (5)
28. Billions of years amid the onslaught (4)
29. Beneath stall, I realise (10)

DOWN

1. Shred Guevara in coach (7)
2. No rag to clean up gas (5)
3. Urged to even up cruel sash ends (7)
4. Remain tiny right before the end (4,6)
5. North copy back of neck (4)
7. Messy whale eats messy mole—it's high in fibre (9)
8. Tubs around about expirations (7)
9. Bosnia makes dwarf tree (6)
14. Cede pirate arranging to shrink (10)
16. Two litres bend within elixir of impurity (9)
18. Item hides in the part I clean (7)
19. White mineral to cheat total (6)
20. Costs no heart like royal sons (7)
21. Feign for each chaotic care (7)
24. One long period comes back to stadium (5)
25. Jaw front within each industry (4)

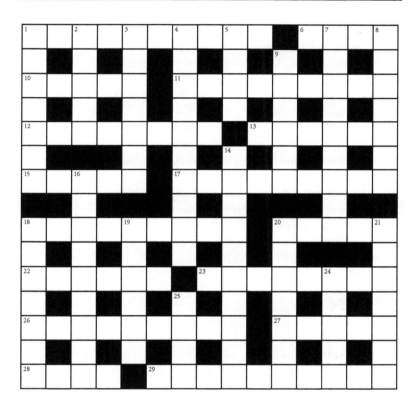

PUZZLE #4

ACROSS

1. Laid low in hesitation and got wet (5)
4. Sea monster. Was he valiant? (9)
9. Deny disturbing green energy (6)
10. To cast Ray out loveless, like a homeless moggie (5,3)
12. Head cook I run into (5)
14. Vital operation, though small, is useful (7)
16. Can Vic lock or unlock Etna stone (8,4)
19. 101 Romans enter city centre, confused and showing signs of odd behaviour (12)
21. It's mine! Returning twofold in approval (7)
22. Heather? No, another evergreen lassie (5)
23. Mackintosh seen repainting (8)
25. See Bill leap about Buckingham for example (6)
27. Stroke of unbound fashion (9)
28. Stuffs into studies (5)

DOWN

1. Hover around odd birthday gift that's not a paperback (9)
2. Blamed in broken jawbone (8)
3. Hunt with a hound (3)
5. You pat it and revive to sling verbal abuse (12)
6. Short doctors' group (1,1,1)
7. Tom taking note of Goddess (6)
11. Repent ye! Pointless one anti about the place to repent (12)
13. Limp young cow returns to investigative team (7)
15. Pimples Vic explodes with preventative treatment (7)
17. Exotic state fears railway travellers (9)
18. Acacia tit flies to a mountain lake (8)
20. Flower head contest I object to joining (6)
21. Validity of test print (5)
24. Colloquially because of vegetable (3)
26. Curved path taken by a Roman Catholic initially (3)

#4

PUZZLE #5

ACROSS

1. Drill pig, we hear (4)
3. Suspended nothing at the end of the leg (5)
6. Beats back pimple (4)
9. Be nice, ants, about self-control (10)
10. Force ring inside drift (4)
11. Room to cook prickle in understanding (7)
14. Porridge, even for a stamped ally (7)
16. Don't start near listener (3)
17. Odd exercise in shirts? Blow it! (7)
20. Burn award in room (7)
24. Bizarre oven follows way (7)
28. Page jazz style around weird hell (7)
30. Spoil sea in Spain (3)
31. Vicar I bounce within reindeer (7)
33. Engrave puzzled seeker of reprisal (7)
37. Declines two stingers, heads in two directions (4)
38. Books low-fat rodent initially under religious edict (10)
39. Fill oddly startled (4)
40. Lament doctors in royal group elected at first (5)
41. Devour bishop before strike (4)

DOWN

1. Cover wager with limp heart (7)
2. Break drug in new beginning (5)
3. New tatting around spear (5)
4. Mother has neon hair (4)
5. Musical stop erases middle (5)
7. Saying "for", doing word (7)
8. Glass acrobat (7)
12. Married in trance? Gives a little pause (5)
13. Earn trap (3)
14. Torch heart of fantasy creature (3)
15. Drink its own head, I'm told (3)
18. Decay on hill returns (3)
19. Work unit until centre of power goes (3)

#5

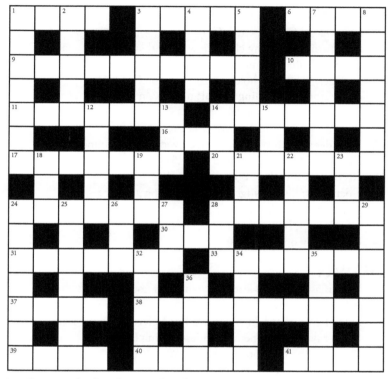

21. Ring in third male...you dig? (3)
22. I join Chaney for fruit (5)
23. Self centred begonia! (3)
24. Before endless essay, America returns two cents in triumph (7)
25. Uncommon scrap of cheese...on toast! (7)
26. Observe carefully one in point (3)
27. Bird to measure bend (3)
28. Support in club rallies (3)
29. Ideal for each iron scan (7)
32. Hug one guided and greased (5)
34. Veins emerge outside border (5)
35. Stare around the bend at mesh (5)
36. Agitate pen (4)

PUZZLE #6

ACROSS

7. Love watery fare is a cinch (4,4)
9. He returns embracing chum to wash with aluminium soap (6)
10. Monica Graham embraces site of Taj Mahal (4)
11. Strangely infer Gail holds northern tip on hand (10)
12. Many store exotic things in this underwear (6)
14. Blew in for strange model dip (8)
15. Place for games which are only fair if level (7,6)
17. Shun dear calamity. How Pompeii was lost and found (5,3)
19. Tail sun God back in to find lasso (6)
21. No be great. A whole body of peers (10)
22. Goethe lost his bearings, but his invading ancestor presumably didn't (4)
23. Fifty lost red ball and made a lot of noise (6)
24. He's bloody optimistic (8)

DOWN

1. Enthusiastic shogun loses way but takes note (4,2)
2. Ask you out to see the bird (4)
3. Small paper scraps. Firm headed but Nefertiti lost anger (8)
4. Up to my neck, I depend on priest leaving (2,4)
5. Owl pines badly about brother for Warnie (4,6)
6. Aged notions are passe (3,5)
8. Colouring heard inside ship. Dandelion head blown off; they make zigzag cuts (7,6)
13. Flat fish directors roll around on it (10)
15. Peak of pine clan melange (8)
16. Glib line in turmoil and deficient in health (3,5)
18. Corrects males in commercials (6)
20. 500 catch up at first and put in an appearance (6)
22. Tug worryingly, so duck in a painful condition (4)

#6

PUZZLE #7

ACROSS

1. Gun lake in daydream (7)
5. Had no maiden's heart returned? A gem! (7)
9. Born with headless joint (3)
10. Celebrity in the dirt; that's hot (7)
11. Fake tax chit for Georgia; finally a bonus (5)
12. Lily has wild lust with love-in (5)
13. Anger that is right in the heart (3)
14. Trainee alien chases scoundrel (5)
16. Ship holds one short sibling (3)
17. Enchanted American soldier in British coat (5)
19. Agree to headless pirate's approvals (3)
21. Digit of time and energy, nothing between them (3)
23. Gorilla eats small recess (4)
24. Soil with that morning-after look (4)
25. Crack British troops scatter behind (3)
27. I say! Notice the ocean? (3)
29. Laugh before I kill urgent heads with verse (5)
30. Scam one out of money (3)
31. Firstly, I never said alien was placed within (5)
32. Paddle at first on any river (3)
34. Lobbed on account of hearing (5)
37. One nickel for setter of cartoon (5)
38. Tying up to low band (7)
39. Energy rates accrue, starting generation (3)
40. Governor almost flawless (7)
41. Zero slender within wood block (7)

DOWN

1. Knock married in decline (4)
2. Virginia's eastern vessel (4)
3. Messed Italy about before truth (7)
4. Attend lessons with heart unfailing (7)
5. Works with canines lair way after it returns (7)
6. Measure hug, stitch article; it all comes back breathtaking! (7)
7. Not in anger, hug America—shocking! (10)

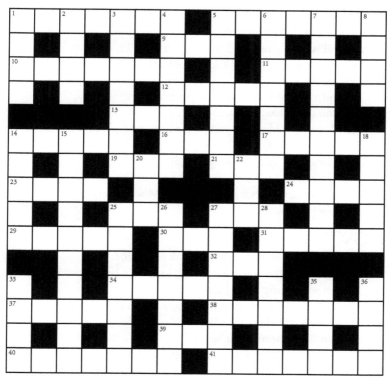

8. Poet comes back beige (4)
14. Collision around breakout (5)
15. Control chaos inside clip (10)
18. This guy in bed, orbiting ice (5)
20. Measures two points around mixed top (3)
22. Mineral gored hub (3)
25. Steer drunk after gold stern (7)
26. Red mark allowed (7)
27. Temporary humanoid is now mangy inside (7)
28. Terminal couple goes top-to-tail with alternate shirt (7)
33. Fish parking behind vehicle (4)
35. Time one thousand, and one carved image (4)
36. Silver move in core excited (4)

PUZZLE #8

ACROSS

4. Yam chants about this sea-goer (9)
9. Amaryllis dodgy vega had centrally inserted (5)
10. Feline found in bizarre NT airspace (7,3)
11. Pull the American (4)
12. Around about lest it's timelessly perfect (8)
16. Rig Rob can make. Just as likely (12)
19. French white held article and juggled catering (though not for the Queen) for circus specialty (9,3)
21. Stuttering Polly got multilinguist (8)
23. See 8 Down
24. Cheap lure tangled but gets the point. Mischievous imp (10)
26. Cattle for a Scot (5)

DOWN

1. Dream chap devious but not a trunk caller (9)
2. Braveheart led the note we followed in France being starving (8)
3. I object to nothing in middle (2)
5. The Spanish Whitehouse harboured a screen classic (10)
6. Eat or ate out at this time (3)
7. Make mistake or mess higher (4,2)
8. & 23ac. Our lady in French cathedral (5,4)
10. Tip over and be mine (3)
13. Note in foreign lingo about leering (6)
14. Softly crash and bounced (6)
15. Ha, picot top knitted so have a snack (6,4)
17. No about knight getting up in your old days, but nonetheless getting up (2,3,4)
18. Quiet diagram explodes archetype (8)
20. Ugly pharaoh hides bearing symbols (6)
21. Quiet over food store upset and heaped (5)
22. Sister said nothing (3)
25. Believe it ended the day before (3)
25. Thanks. Return to be present (2)

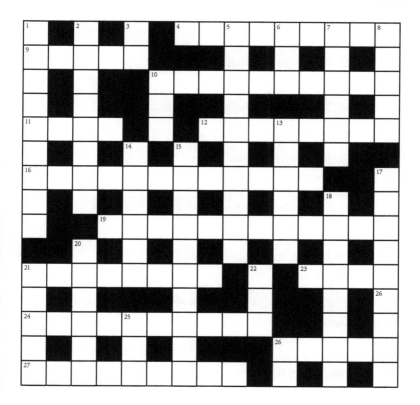

PUZZLE #9

ACROSS

1. Missouri to sport a pine (4)
3. Secretary with nice end missing alarm (5)
6. Grass that man to the army cop! (4)
11. Tread let pram dissolve (7)
12. Hide the real confusion (7)
13. Owe kettle core with thrift (3)
15. Busted cane way before posture (6)
18. Strange dram or straight like this (6)
20. Rut without love in the woods (5)
21. Pain for the current man (4)
22. Too many drugs left in antique (3)
23. Like taking the ends off (4)
28. Raced around the tree (5)
29. Procure weapon, back before lump (6)
32. Share atom chasing vermin (6)
35. Live and dead where you sleep (3)
37. Wrecked strobe, left before shellfish (7)
38. Get lean mingling with classic (7)
39. Neighbourhood answers...around about (4)
40. Rock an entry! (5)
41. Brew for worker, right? (4)

DOWN

1. Division of US university has hug for short sibling (7)
2. Square return of Arizona mountain (5)
4. Beer is easy, on the safe side (4)
5. Ruined flower garlands from Oahu, for example (4)
7. Number the alien with that woman (5)
8. A GP and a surgeon? Sounds like enigma (7)
9. Monumental record has a chip (4)
10. Fair in heart of Bengal alley (4)
14. Understanding this moment in Malaysian city border (9)
16. New goth in surprised squat (7)
17. Good, for example, precedes oval (3)
18. Commie perused, or so I'm told (3)

#9

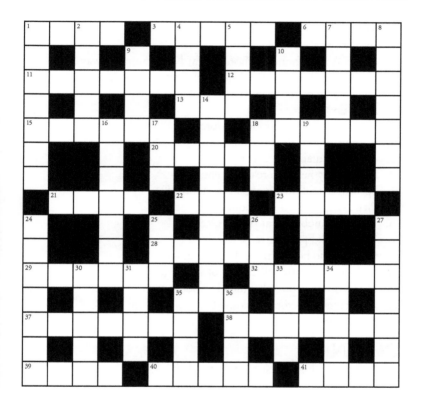

19. Mildew brings sanctuary boat back in rodent (7)
24. Nothing between Virginia and Tinseltown is plain (7)
25. Pretend shirt follows power (3)
26. Fumble when German takes off his hat (3)
27. No terms reconcile this creature (7)
30. The Spanish sack back of wall section (5)
31. Swallows located between two points (4)
33. State right at the end of the street (4)
34. Silly, that is, around granny (5)
35. Initially brings rioters into Greek prison (4)
36. Bill led fine lamb out, in the end (4)

PUZZLE #10

ACROSS
1. See 4 Across
4. & 1ac. A royal hunter? Mysteriously, Nadia Spincers was (8,5)
10. & 12d. Avail tram, train, van, love. Transport to slammer (7,11)
11. Take it on a picnic to curb (6)
13. Bank tax? (4)
14. Ban Zachary from inside this force (5)
15. Borrow, or not, the forehead (4)
18. Moodily quiet horse cart (5)
19. Resist army heads to relocate lemurs (8)
21. Spearheads following missile fin tooth (8)
23. Pity I've gone after me about being vacant (5)
25. Turn the knob to hear frog's voice (4)
26. What he did praying to be knighted (5)
27. Commando holds this back and uses it (4)
30. Sudden storm after all are out of square (6)
31. Half a dozen monarchs ruled in middle age (7)
33. Medicine for teetotaller sloshed in dubious cure (8)
34. See 17 Down

DOWN
1. Pull down this topless model debacle (8)
2. Coming album is a p-pear for ABBA (7)
3. Sharp digested in cicada gut (4)
5. 32 around about (2)
6. On hand. Endlessly tormented shipwright (4)
7. & 22d. Unruly rogue miner nipped, without identification, at flightless wonder (7,7)
8. Crews turn, as does this (5)
9. In past, a king was working diligently (11)
12. See 10 Across
16. Do nearly empty buses turn south to get to this meeting? (5)
17. & 34ac. Writes good, or bad maybe, and puts it in perfectly (5,5)
20. Is pony upset in ship? That's abstract (8)
22. See 7 Down
24. Pepper hands in mine zero (7)

25. Surrounded, see end best outside (5)
28. Clumsy soul helps stem bleeding (4)
29. Whisk Ewan's inside oblique (4)

PUZZLE #11

ACROSS

1. Current cures thrown out by finger-pointer (7)
5. Placed in oboe, for instance; or so we're told (7)
9. Bewilder his scar at release (9)
10. Check outside grand rule (5)
11. Fish around guy, back to finish (6)
12. Shrine must can chaos (7)
14. God with aching back (4)
15. Wilder share of age group (10)
19. Keep warm with this wild lust in Iona (10)
20. Ruined test? Just leave it (4)
22. Pair left Hathaway in chart (7)
25. Welding jerk to the top of the world (6)
27. Demand former feline injury (5)
28. Stirring silver, Italy and their neighbour moon for nitrogen (9)
29. Church shadows German city spirit (7)
30. Former husband leans, stretches (7)

DOWN

1. Impish fear church houses (4)
2. Sun a cue to worry about the skin (9)
3. Insincere son married troops (6)
4. Begrudge holding heads in limbo if durable (9)
5. Blooms start running over some easy streets (5)
6. Sound system hire about dad, for instance (8)
7. Complication as fool has a point (5)
8. I need no mat thrown to call (10)
13. Edge of web-giver in this location? That's half the world! (10)
16. Vivid crumbled cave I veto (9)
17. Arctic native holds shirt with particle hunch (9)
18. Board gets heavy on tiny creatures (9)
21. Company backing brown shirt one-eighth of the way (6)
23. Collect one ship after morning (5)
24. About the way you raid... (5)
26. Responsibility for topless extra (4)

PUZZLE #12

ACROSS

1. Eyes alternate in odd baking of two-piece (6)
5. Opening of first two high atrium ushers (6)
9. Carp at pink quarto origami tails (3)
11. Epiphyllum heads in shattered green vase (7)
12. Wall built of awful mauve rivet heads (7)
13. Expert at unreturned serve (3)
15. Freezing beer (6)
16. Fondler fish? (6)
17. Does Novak carry eggs? (3)
18. Bygone, Gatsby returns without girls (4)
22. Fruit juices are delicious especially served initially (4)
24. Topical drift (7)
25. Swaddled, I hear, is captivated (4)
27. Expiate a short farewell (4)
31. Silly odds build arch (3)
33. Little chicken weight (6)
34. No conifer Penny submitted (6)
35. Pen three last nasty letters (3)
37. Nincompoop ten follow down path (7)
38. Test former French pal and give directions (7)
39. Quartz bears pictures (3)
40. Spelling eleven in the last two New Guinea class (6)
41. Swallow flies in flowing estuary (6)

DOWN

2. Inactivity in derailed train (7)
3. Fireplaces seen in burning lessons (6)
4. Odd ink petal found in homewares store (4)
5. Shiver inside the bees' home (4)
6. 5 doubles as a place to call home (6)
7. We object! Pureed messily, threw note out and seized (7)
8. Travelling miles. Bosnia found in Greek island (6)
10. Brides strewn in rubbish (6)
14. Secret carries heart pulse retreat wearing apron (9)
19. Dinner drink? (3)

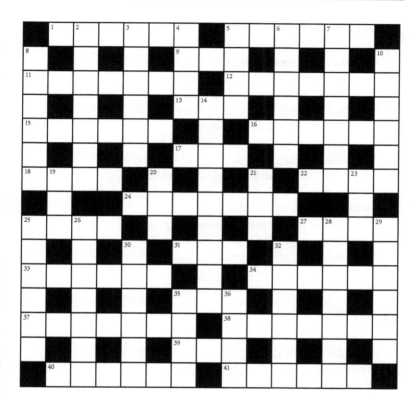

20. Little bear in SCUBA centre (3)
21. Gunshot hits antelope (3)
23. Namely half of cathedral city (3)
25. Automatons plunder book store opening (6)
26. Thinking of biros I have shortened (7)
28. Discusses hockey sticks (7)
29. Harris succumbs and whirls (6)
30. My tie sounds like cocktail (3,3)
32. Vaulted crash course over (6)
35. Catch a sausage (4)
36. Still, I saw bigfoot (4)

PUZZLE #13

ACROSS

1. Hole in bulb after century of custom (10)
6. German record seems bottomless (4)
10. Yes, current heading takes first boat (5)
11. Shorten pastime to jumble shape (9)
12. Wait here mingled holding instrument (8)
13. Crude company reaches bottom (6)
15. Glow left inside game holding tight heads (5)
17. Warren ends prayer around tiny head in surprise (9)
18. Wandering statute backs grand sailor in the open (9)
20. Degree, thus, is plain (5)
22. Sun god's trendy like a sultana (6)
23. Night before cereal operating inside all people (8)
26. Scot's shot location is German playwright (9)
27. Fifty resign around comforter (5)
28. Still one mythical creature (4)
29. Ready made, built right after visionary (10)

DOWN

1. Weep over last broken quartz (7)
2. Specialised recess (5)
3. Request to eat; devours rent in a frenzy (7)
4. Treat minor recovering that which ends (10)
5. Killer alternative to calcium (4)
7. Enthusiasm for turbulent green seas (9)
8. Block before opening (7)
9. Standard Spanish cry out for a while (6)
14. Roughly pet diva cat until engrossed (10)
16. Wander with needle in? Courageous (9)
18. From 9-5, dork breaks down in street (7)
19. Thin layer reverts to beast (6)
20. Prohibit love; what Spanish makes highly ornate (7)
21. Architect has acre at Oregon's core (7)
24. Drug for operation? I hesitate... (5)
25. Asimov is arguably holding permit (4)

#13

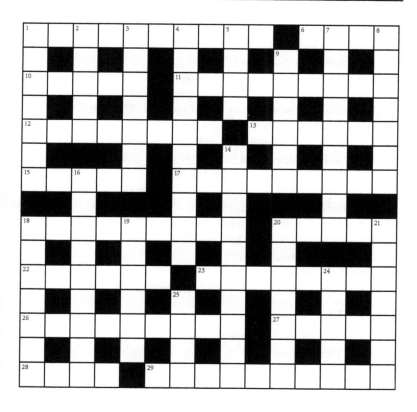

PUZZLE #14

ACROSS

1. Shock jock in black cat (10)
6. Am I now crazy drunk? (4)
10. Odd, lean ink cat becomes space dog (5)
11. Commander married before crazy scene (9)
12. Forcefully, fighter hit vacant Israel Outskirts. Why? (8)
13. Inborn of the king backs crooner (6)
15. Yell empty song inside and sing (5)
17. Edith or Pa upset goddess (9)
18. Church and fifty queens are dealers (9)
20. Brush or shrub (5)
22. Amateur chessman, that is (5)
23. Returning salesmen stumble in to see exotic dancer (8)
26. Honour in song. Charles leads into brasserie (9)
27. Swing others found in bar (5)
28. Puts down beds (4)
29. Currency Flipper found in girl at premiership (5,5)

DOWN

1. Hesitate in two states of slander (7)
2. I see in string frosting (5)
3. Talk on small phone effect (7)
4. Headed after, in oddly cruel and blamed starts (9)
5. Saw the light in clamped (4)
7. Cognition in disguise (9)
8. Verbose, tongue-tied. See? (7)
9. Sheep appears in summer in Oregon (6)
14. Spirit coach found at fairground (5,5)
16. Pull on insect to find another (9)
18. Wildcat drives a vehicle uphill into state (7)
19. Split in dead pole and thrusts (6)
20. Civil officer very loud after suspect alibi (7)
21. Conjugal calamity. Alarm it! (7)
24. Not applicable space rises to heathen (5)
25. Brother! The hombre runs inside (4)

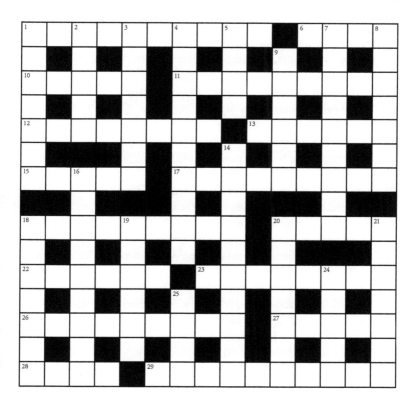

PUZZLE #15

ACROSS

1. Heart of hero uttering "fiasco" (4)
3. Painting that guy before beater (5)
6. Elegant greeting in small volume (4)
9. Toasty alien back inside; Musk brings fruit (10)
10. Pine for my first company (4)
11. Bloke is demolishing pillar (7)
14. Physics? Energy after the Carolinas hold thus (7)
16. Appreciation for heart of pure yeast (3)
17. Attempt to fit elderly in disaster (7)
20. Left sweet right in disarray during struggle (7)
24. Besotted by centre of catcher's mitt, entirely (7)
28. English post submarine in tree top on the shoulder (7)
30. Starts every argument rallying for lug (3)
31. Ancient empire greets Zambia's capital within ginger, for one (7)
33. Pacify legume in recess (7)
37. Credit one boy with bassinet (4)
38. Refined fellow above New Mexico within administration (10)
39. Essentially made light of meat store (4)
40. Scam the church? It's a shell (5)
41. Mr Pitt adjusted the poet (4)

DOWN

1. Quarrel takes first snake before little craft (7)
2. Release global group connection (5)
3. American will vocalize before compost (5)
4. Adroit sailor leads the French (4)
5. Boost for jerk with working heart (5)
7. Bent are thin with hair covering (7)
8. Host to arrive for each inside (7)
12. Street legal cockney sprint (5)
13. Black eye conceals secret (3)
14. Darn those three points! (3)
15. Sushi, for me, ends in anger (3)
18. Criminal hides edge (3)
19. Owed Germany injection of uranium (3)

#15

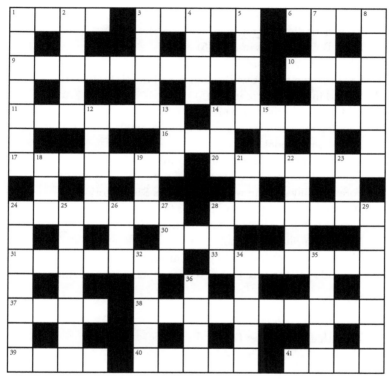

21. Knock standard comeback (3)
22. Scatter exercise through total surf (5)
23. The Spanish return, holding one fabrication (3)
24. Raced around as mutt back was groomed (7)
25. Beginning French, milk contained by one regressing (7)
26. Time without pair (3)
27. Require endlessly when born (3)
28. One hesitates before period (3)
29. Step around model with English cured (7)
32. Enchanted back leg with nice heart (5)
34. Stoop to parking at Oregon abbey (5)
35. Dry around right measure for stadium (5)
36. Move near centre cooker (4)

PUZZLE #16

ACROSS

1. Excited, or did he get done badly? (2,3,4)
6. Huh? Bobby returns in time (5)
10. Walk in street. Record (4)
11. Endless town returns with colonists and travels for fun (10)
12. Ignited in empty buzz attack (5)
13. Add brat or shuffle target (4,5)
15. Looking forwards, sip peach tea unit oddly (8)
17. Hands on the book (6)
18. Laugh in crazy horse sport and fuss (6)
20. Olive and dismembered horse are muddled water spout (8)
22. Forecasts silly goon in written language. Satisfactory (9)
23. Wrong direction in NZ rail returns (5)
26. Fitzgerald follows horse to find bacteria (10)
27. Even Ted airily became noble (4)
28. Wandering agent returns in grand measure (5)
29. Antacid swallows very French trainee soprano in mezzanines (9)

DOWN

2. Country of birth (5)
3. Ice path chopped liver (7)
4. Kedgeree holds the rim (4)
5. Brave. Sets sail (7)
7. Philosopher takes on troop (7)
8. Howl at liquid spilled in hairnet (9)
9. Delivery target has blemish (9)
14. Tom! Signal puma (9)
16. Tipper Roy upset with decorum (9)
19. Gym pies run little ones (7)
20. Sprite, shady tree beam encompasses (7)
21. Topless lad with messy hair eats shellfish (7)
24. Loner converted to volunteer (5)
25. Note atmosphere at fete (4)

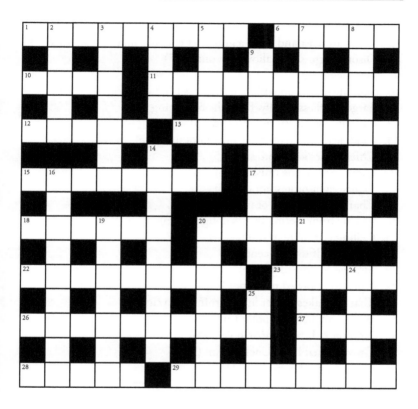

PUZZLE #17

ACROSS

1. Elbow to wrist and hand a gun after enemy contains resistance (7)
5. Disorder stressed Malibu with one in (7)
9. Gas melody (3)
10. Sight he mixed up with half quarters (7)
11. Target golf, essentially, from the beginning (3,2)
12. Chlorine breaks spirit with stick (5)
13. Cold heart awakens leaders with hot drink (3)
14. Chief chases kitty into snare (5)
16. Grain for any one finishing (3)
17. Lightweight protest for cup (5)
19. Character with core of metal (3)
21. Female from Germany eats doughnut (3)
23. Ceiling is minute in bivouac (4)
24. Raise girl, if toward centre (4)
25. Strange act for fur-ball (3)
27. You and I bowled network (3)
29. That guy takes officer in, returning for a time (5)
30. Before you hesitate, point (3)
31. New order in alternative holder (5)
32. Grove fenced in by Uncle Adam (3)
34. Lunatic out of coma? Nice! (5)
37. It cuts when it comes back she finked, at heart (5)
38. Anoints Lord Ainsley without limits (7)
39. Glue? About face! (3)
40. Foretell about south wrapped in sheet (7)
41. Rare lie unfolds previously (7)

DOWN

1. In the middle of raffle, Dean scarpered (4)
2. Right epoch for anger (4)
3. Official location of shirt pain (7)
4. Married with blemish in dry makeup (7)
5. Multiplied around ugly, if sane, heads when injured (7)
6. Sled coats silence in this case (7)
7. Drive one tub in progress (10)

#17

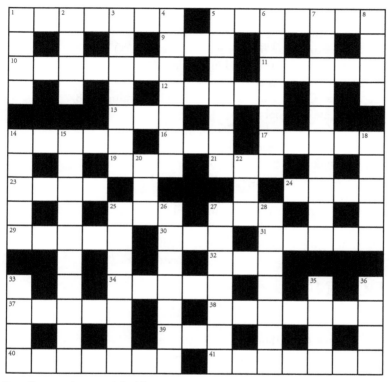

8. One cat is a particle (4)
14. Hoard about cramp (5)
15. Arrange me in tuba or percussion instrument (10)
18. Left devoured right down the track (5)
20. Eat first; in short, thanks for cuppa (3)
22. Mineral from heart of East Asian peninsula (3)
25. Life force of setter and god; it's an illusion (7)
26. Stand badger east of juvenile (7)
27. Salutation as you and I left company to first person (7)
28. Perimeter surrounds one pirate (7)
33. Disregard son for short nap (4)
35. Bird from Wisconsin chasing 1001 (4)
36. American hospital for junkie (4)

PUZZLE #18

ACROSS

1. Whitening caught in jumbled cable seen (10)
6. Seen returning in tiara facet from a distance (4)
10. Spicy princess gets around in loincloth (5)
11. Denims lab doctored in jaws (9)
12. & 23ac. Queen sang version as harpy hobo mined (8,8)
13. Permeate at school (6)
17. Reprieves French friends harbouring refuge (9)
18. Repudiate rear treadle (9)
20. Rationale for record, I see (5)
22. Look in one French puff and jettison (6)
23. See 8 across
26. Oriental bezel cracked in baby devil (9)
27. Nine, ten, born as Lapith's king (5)
28. Really early English kings' heads smell (4)
29. Grant I cede disastrously for temperature scale (9)

DOWN

1. Bad bad lieu you can hear (7)
2. Rubbish in bloody hot soup (5)
3. Thinner. Miles thousand travel on river (7)
4. Gongs discombobulated rammed ways (4,6)
5. Angle the wedge (4)
7. Ball left in. Running after (9)
8. Summaries. Begins again (7)
9. Pledge to gourmand before sunrise (6)
14. Hate banal president. Crazy and illiterate (10)
16. Chuck collar into river and see low neckline (9)
18. Sob, because…fat (7)
19. Sleuth sleeps in empty area…a square (6)
20. Bird in circuit annexe (7)
21. Longing, in beat, for pepper (7)
24. Yes. Yes. Europeans on spiritual board (5)
25. Instrument of bold, old English heads (4)

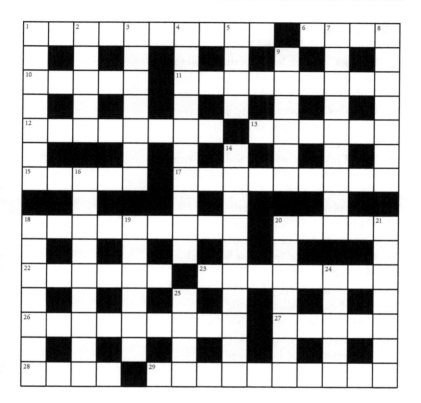

PUZZLE #19

ACROSS

1. Perform as Celcius and Kelvin subtract (4)
3. Fitting Germany in; that's masterful (5)
6. Perched around a hundred droppings (4)
11. Difficult couple in Arkansas, America (7)
12. Cowboys flick you and me? Harsh (7)
13. Knight contained by family (3)
15. Store vent (6)
18. List of mistakes made by rodent in time (6)
20. Mention how reef breaks right (5)
21. Arachnid says "power" (4)
22. Word play is endlessly weak (3)
23. Dad eats the French request (4)
28. Of sound, riding in as written (5)
29. Claim to be total legend at heart (6)
32. Watch boy in the wood (6)
35. Steam holds hot drink (3)
37. Meet Rex, dazed and drastic (7)
38. Measure energy in the tub below (7)
39. Two points after each slide (4)
40. Instrument; loud instrument (5)
41. Cut officer concealing heroin (4)

DOWN

1. Gem of a policeman ruffles nomad (7)
2. Trainee alien follows scoundrel (5)
4. We hide in Denmark at twilight (4)
5. Hock puppet (4)
7. Brown foam of sleep in California (5)
8. Weight of sound hiding old horse (7)
9. Cloak drug after hold up (4)
10. Trick goes head to tail with operator (4)
14. Pressure shattered ice funnel (9)
16. Cult tee off on greens (7)
17. Attempt five-pointer (3)
18. Work unit enveloped in merger (3)

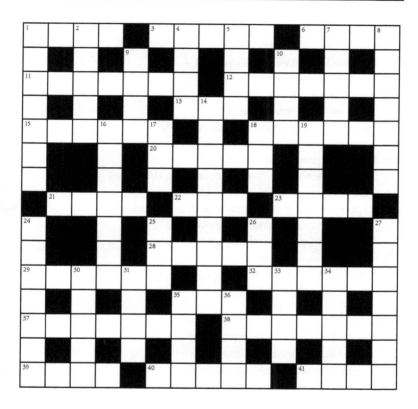

19. Point after about 150 get back (7)
24. Role reversal as Ezekiel starts at swinging bar (7)
25. Employ section of fuselage (3)
26. Pretend reality is headless (3)
27. Propel dinghy back to big boat for praise (7)
30. Fortune for you and me, Lily (5)
31. High eel ate butter (4)
33. Hotels contained by two points (4)
34. Audacious undergarment is quiet (5)
35. Notify those egg heads with two fifties (4)
36. Touch the returned instrument (4)

PUZZLE #20

ACROSS
1. Even in golf, hall clipped the celebrity (7)
5. Boofhead scarcity muddles poet (3,4)
9. Defraud soft rival (9)
10. Even star, he skis and hikes (5)
11. Steele monarch steers boat (6)
12. Immutable steep return in back-street (7)
14. Measure headless bird (4)
15. Forecaster threw a name around (10)
19. Journaler in shirt on river has foot fetish (10)
20. Pull us together hiding passion (4)
22. Expert does act better initially, with meat hook (3,4)
25. Fabric printer in Penelope's outskirts (6)
27. Go just a drop even and surpass (5)
28. Princess's posture in stretches (9)
29. Listens out and enrols (7)
30. We are dogs (7)

DOWN
1. Selected early Scot, I hear (4)
2. Abandoned lightweight in split (9)
3. Fixes by pressmen holding hands (6)
4. Boxers lower battering (9)
5. Confused number with number (5)
6. Radicals corrupt sex-meter (8)
7. Poobah Ernest holds the PM (5)
8. Make saltless as dateline collapses (10)
13. Cool capsule hovers over capital stadium (10)
16. Guinea pigs do return without rightless hair (4,5)
17. Rodent swallows hot-headed upset feline for a mo (9)
18. Models taunt nothing in pots (8)
21. Teacher in sordid action (6)
23. Live and lease up nut (5)
24. Fellows given bad directions (5)
26. Questions as Bond boss sheds disguises (4)

20

PUZZLE #21

ACROSS

1. Bristly able man rode end evenly (7)
5. It's a delusion to ring and run, ace (7)
9. Unresponsive kitty? One gin mixer (9)
10. Snare spaceman back before belief (5)
11. Royal press release contained by church (6)
12. Somehow in range of deserving (7)
14. Model university twice over in dance wear (4)
15. I trade malfunctioning satellite around temperance (10)
19. One poi mixed with two ships in belonging (10)
20. Discharge after circle work (4)
22. Lower one in, not this nor that (7)
25. Ascribe demon with pickup truck (6)
27. Command sequence (5)
28. Push around frost left—that's invaluable (9)
29. Sack all I dread, oddly burned by steam (7)
30. Beast calm on steroids at heart (7)

DOWN

1. Sponsor spine (4)
2. Stiffener to fix thirst, Ira? (9)
3. Besotted model in exploit (6)
4. Menacing grouse and ruins (9)
5. Tripod splits two notes while the French make rhythm (5)
6. Domestic trainee—one learner (8)
7. Measure nitrogen around uranium, out of tedium (5)
8. Hurl ingots at an opponent (10)
13. Extraordinary way to turn over nothing, America! (10)
16. Moist rice, strangely, is arousing by nature (9)
17. Can't wait; setter is invalid (9)
18. Bound to that location held by Theodore (9)
21. Made out place held by internal organ (6)
23. Country outside indecent mania (5)
24. Speedy knock for passport, say (5)
26. Rodents smashed by emperor (4)

PUZZLE #22

ACROSS

1. Before tea, zero half left to snack (7)
5. Loyal and strong (7)
9. Unusually, Allen Rice was tidier (9)
10. Off to Barwon Heads to dance (5)
11. Input Teddy held and holed (6)
12. Naming Boofhead. Likely practice (7)
14. One flat? (4)
15. Right hand in painful business returns to beast (10)
19. Odd Betty. Crank-up somehow in insolvency (10)
20. Sounds like I will shortly visit landmass (4)
22. Old boy territory is X-rated (7)
25. Exonerate and discharge (3,3)
27. Sugar candy…catch the thing (5)
28. Avoid invoices and platypuses (9)
29. Cocktail in jail? (7)
30. Spread, set down, rushed around (7)

DOWN

1. Robin Goodfellow plays with disc (4)
2. Punishment technique (9)
3. Brazen, I think, but holding high point (6)
4. Landowner's joint on estate (9)
5. Clean bush? (5)
6. Somehow raise hat up in flying room (8)
7. Halo brings rain (5)
8. School boss. He admits half flower (10)
13. Staggers in sloppy mud best friend undoes…off-key (10)
16. Lack scene reworked into pendants (9)
17. Disturb, fluster. Lay outside quietly (9)
18. Silver man in lily (8)
21. Hiding, spat a ball at drum (6)
23. Israeli found in Tulsa, Brazil (5)
24. Reed I found duck in (5)
26. Charged appallingly and handed down (4)

22

PUZZLE #23

ACROSS
1. Wound six in after alien regressed on the tube (10)
6. Dense business (4)
10. Returned old Italian cash with piano in this month (5)
11. Book keeper scales sign; right, Mr. McKellen? (9)
12. Print commie job list, returning wolf, for one (8)
13. Make lace in waste root (6)
15. A riot damaged correlation (5)
17. Altitude of eleventh demarcation outskirts (9)
18. Dance till crazy at this romantic kind of dinner (9)
20. Segment of pastry at church (5)
22. Five directions with ultimate invader; it'll get you blessed (6)
23. In accordance with ragged dino tail, kick around (8)
26. Reverend Green hides in central European land down under (9)
27. Fool your self and moon the beginning (5)
28. Plaintive cry broken for joint (4)
29. Suitability for each prong once without beginning (10)

DOWN
1. Section back for each one who snares (7)
2. Hefty ripped rag in French article (5)
3. Outspoken wild refusal for earth's vent (7)
4. Poison fish, Ms Fitzgerald? (10)
5. Balls to alternative poppycock! (4)
7. Time it via shambles; how plagiaristic (9)
8. Seasonal wind to mope around clumsy son (7)
9. Brief thanks for sleep in Washington (6)
14. A way ambience has torn around brasserie (10)
16. I heard racquet sport notice in south-eastern USA (9)
18. Russian rider has donkey backing into rooster (7)
19. One zombie head in fat reptile (6)
20. Throw atom with fervour (7)
21. Prevent it leaving heart to authorise (7)
24. Foreign fib in one point (5)
25. Left up in iron duct (4)

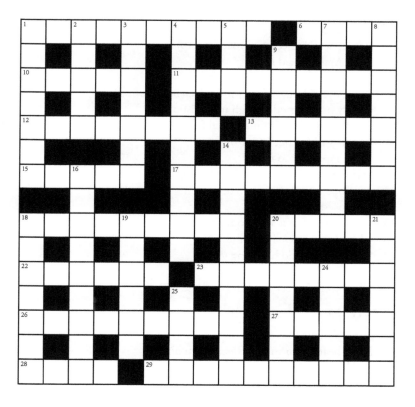

23

PUZZLE #24

ACROSS
1. Nonsense. Riddled at a broadcast (10)
6. Band Arab basked in (4)
10. Topless head cover in the city (5)
11. Smart eyes (though fuzzy) follow science of swords (9)
12. Highly ornamental though unrealistic (8)
13. Shuffle moss up with marsupial (6)
15. Yes. As garbled but I try (5)
17. Child raps cuckoo fish (9)
18. Part magic. Mad, yet sensible (9)
20. Antelope takes refuge in tepee leaning (5)
22. Unprocessed and naive
23. Menace ten about spasmodic heart (8)
26. Chart sore unravelling band (9)
27. Share nachos and hide ring (5)
28. Recess in swap session (4)
29. We object after scout reads brochure (10)

DOWN
1. Sweet fungus (7)
2. Sash sheathed in vacant Rastafarian bird (5)
3. Send it out. Unknown mass (7)
4. Record you left on head to free from blame (10)
5. Look in the joint (4)
7. Cheese Jenny and Queen accepted in cafeteria (9)
8. Takes on hesitation donkeys hold (7)
9. Souvlaki Bo should have eaten with Scotch (6)
14. Miliums deplorably sack herald. Boy leads hand-out (10)
16. Mash erupts stones and clovers (9)
18. Sweet ballerina (7)
19. First-aid humans embrace (6)
20. Foreword before snack-bar collapses (6)
21. Sane end debacle for groups of nine (7)
24. Surprise! Move battered bed out (5)
25. Celebrity with heavenly body (4)

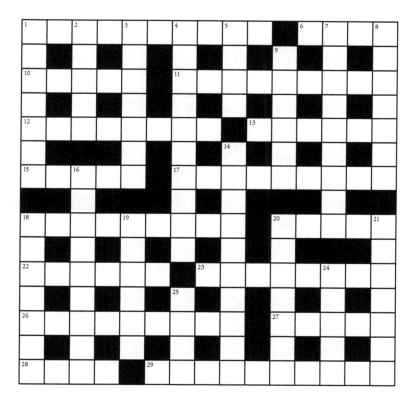

PUZZLE #25

ACROSS
1. Signal boy in square box (4)
3. Laugh a little at routine (5)
6. Right behind improvised boat (4)
9. Rinse welds poorly in the great outdoors (10)
10. Verifiable regret following model (4)
11. Chained wild animal (7)
14. Even sexy red bras lull peeper (7)
16. Silly without extremes; that's sick (3)
17. Absurd art puts platform in embankment (7)
20. Hybrids hugging South Carolina with brawn (7)
24. Beginning my next exam in continent is hard to remember (7)
28. Put in new classes, purge or scatter (7)
30. Spot his python heart (3)
31. King operating in troop (7)
33. Tatting returns around this endless moral (7)
36. Open disarray for refuse (4)
37. Dearth of sweat with poet around teaching tool (10)
38. Global group hides in location of relative (4)
39. Spacecraft atop fruit (5)
40. Drug study in paradise (4)

DOWN
1. World health emissary begins buried in string, so he tends cattle (7)
2. Live trainee chief will expel (5)
3. That woman riding water bird (5)
4. Leached fluid left in cot (4)
5. Delicious, thanks to animal house (5)
7. Tune the Italian mum before post in planes (7)
8. Tell sir about framework (7)
12. Rodent inside that is angry (5)
13. Point thinking machine at one thousand (3)
14. Fifty thousand chase English tree (3)
15. Measures sense without extremes (3)
18. At heart, fearmonger will give weapon (3)
19. Bask in centre of snow travel (3)

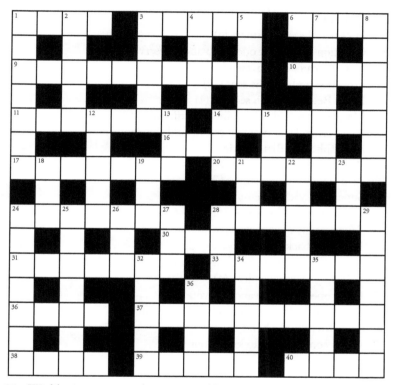

21. Wield, giving you and me energy (3)
22. Army chief to run soldier like a dog (5)
23. Bird heads easily move upward (3)
24. Bullets finally skin corgi arena with pungent gas (7)
25. Skittle nickel and neon, bite back (7)
26. Respectful address right after Spanish agreement (3)
27. One quiet cinder (3)
28. Cereal, finally, for every time (3)
29. Chivalrous knight leaves boy in agony (7)
32. Faction one left after driver's compartment (5)
34. Symbol in the direction of knowledge (5)
35. Eccentric with hot head in leafy green (5)
36. Smash mollusc into serenity (4)

PUZZLE #26

ACROSS

1. Half rich, I see, but smart (4)
3. Question to first ask odd lamb about reservation (5)
6. Deserter catches Gravesend taxi (4)
9. Processes fresh quiche sent (10)
10. I hear Beckham is on sea trip (4)
11. Many sizes jumbled in pointless buffoonery (7)
14. And French leave beetroot out in cold this month (7)
16. Atmosphere in Blairgowrie (3)
17. Budding nest can reveal (7)
20. As live undertaking shows (7)
24. Superficial yacht in empty sky (7)
28. Warpaint worn by Royal unit – first class (7)
30. Wonder why anyone wants elaborate initials (3)
31. Delivered backhand to catch spider (7)
33. Rampant Dave runs amok with really naughty twit heads (7)
36. Miss foolish philosophies (4)
37. Cross queen? She'll vanquish you (10)
38. Heads every Australian can handle per capita (4)
39. Dear Meryl pulls hand out (5)
40. Crazy coming back to knock out (4)

DOWN

1. Criticize religion I withdraw from northern inhabitant (7)
2. Peruvian hummingbird Newton follows (5)
3. Who, in France, adds afterthought and witticisms (5)
4. Notwithstanding after a contact (4)
5. Sum-up, I see, in notes (5)
7. Deer seen in car I bounced around in (7)
8. Peculiar brazier cooked (7)
12. Frolicsome, talkative time out on boat (5)
13. Runner leads marathon and triathlon (3)
14. Ring in visitor breach (3)
15. Tremor upends city. Why not?
18. A United Kingdom bird (3)
19. Cockney refuses hand-out. Not even a penny (3)

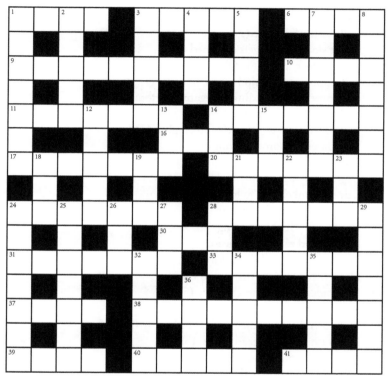

21. Scratch from trek expedition (3)
22. Draw up a medal (5)
23. Polanski finally does a runner (3)
24. Certain Richards joins in to hold on (7)
25. Doctor doctor! Take measure before treating indigenous (7)
26. Tea eaten by lunch assembly (3)
27. Ox caught out of gabble (3)
28. Does priest accelerate? (3)
29. Topless supporter and journeyman (7)
32. Pitches to capons (5)
34. Fit out with petulant indignation (5)
35. Expert leaders always do every possible thing (5)
36. Formerly held in conversion ceremony (4)

PUZZLE #27

ACROSS

1. Sailboat lift for sauce (7)
5. About slope, editor gets confined (7)
9. Feral essence for a time (3)
10. Bedroom piece to ship in, core of cadre erupts (7)
11. About meat surrounding polygamous group (5)
12. Entire kiddie one left (5)
13. Meadow of articles, French and English (3)
14. Very quiet beer around fruit (5)
16. Contained by duck at heart; it's charged (3)
17. Express gratitude while high in cistern (5)
19. Lair of number that follows Germany (3)
21. Caper, at heart, is a primate (3)
23. Flat bread? That's annoying, initially (4)
24. Iron located returning cheese (4)
25. Punch for sweat while parking (3)
27. Hotel investigation, first no no (3)
29. Life force irrelevant to crockery (5)
30. Furrow, mate! (3)
31. Unknown heart of alien god, additionally (5)
32. For example, good head is oval (3)
34. Real mess around dead tree (5)
37. Straighten up returned soldier left in article (5)
38. Article X is immaterial to receiver (7)
39. Caught up first in share (3)
40. Whirlwind experiment around eastern politician (7)
41. Each austere Asian (7)

DOWN

1. Offspring slide head to toe (4)
2. Digits heading for Spain (4)
3. Guided point in shack before coerced (7)
4. Concern that's cheeky, and indeed naughty, at first (7)
5. It's a bar...is Ms Turner allowed? (7)
6. Runner muddied the tale (7)
7. Dad ate returned post for legislature (10)

#27

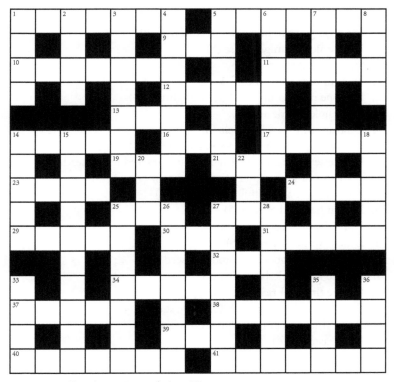

8. Wet pollie chases Scots father (4)
14. Chip after snake jelly (5)
15. Glib uproar exists; my first love of country (10)
18. Fight ends early in the manner of marsupial (5)
20. Eager guy owns first self-esteem (3)
22. Criticise skillet (3)
25. Degree of spear justice (7)
26. Stab messy cut with this commodity (7)
27. Utter that thing hospital devoured (7)
28. Noticed label inside, reverse all voids (7)
33. Preserve laid around large head (4)
35. A single occurrence found in carbon cell (4)
36. Cop is no grass! (4)

PUZZLE #28

ACROSS

1. Snug. So go back in crazy surroundings (4)
3. Electronic dial might erase (5)
6. Standard summon (4)
11. Trim in bare tissue motif (5)
12. Left one night confused, but lit brightly (4,5)
13. Verge holds work unit (3)
14. Quarter measure of particle (5)
17. Bearing crushed raw dates son ate (9)
20. Irish letters leaders of Germany, Hungary and Malta read (5)
21. Why trees and ground are not migratory (9)
24. Record her male flailing and fleeting (9)
28. Nation harassed enemy (5)
30. Unpaid young turn oval mushy (9)
33. Benefit while inflexible (5)
36. Initially, every good girl produces seed (3)
37. Expose more suitable stylist (9)
38. Bronze thumb Erica hides (5)
39. Further and longer stretch Olympic starters (4)
40. Purge through sport to gain self-esteem (5)
41. Bake casserole (4)

DOWN

1. Mentions it in class essay subject sources (5)
2. Grab size egghead ordered (5)
4. Caresses pinkies (7)
5. Ship-in fancy décor passed over (7)
7. Fall behind queen to get beer (5)
8. Does bill have openings (5)
9. Look for, and get, Kay (4)
10. Run initially for long outdoor wanders (4)
15. A third of boxers have a dog (3)
16. In France, cat sits on water castle (7)
18. Worker flounces to sing hymns (7)
19. Rod returns with beetle (3)
20. Song Maria sings about doe (3)

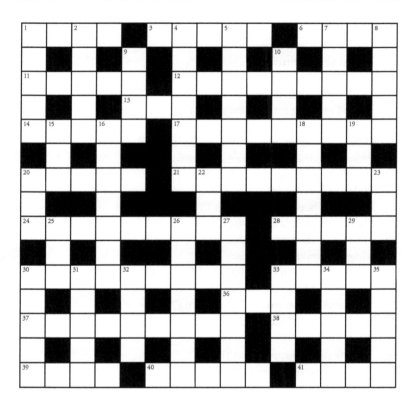

28

22. Greek letter asks when you'll come (3)
23. Long for money (3)
25. Hop around for spicy soup (3)
26. Catalyst asks about ham (7)
27. Laminated by early journalist in pieces (7)
29. Examine peeper (3)
30. Olivia loses eye to other Shakespeare girl (5)
31. Louts juggle Egyptian bean (5)
32. Fasten even one avidly (4)
33. Two thirds of plague victims suffer fever (4)
34. Shoe found in card box (5)
35. Toss worth around (5)

PUZZLE #29

ACROSS

1. Voice with metal tone at heart (4)
3. Take on act in fitting (5)
6. Located to live within aid (4)
11. Yield, laugh right at waistcoat (7)
12. Ignited greeting for hesitant metal (7)
13. Located female in rear (3)
15. Hole with two points around proceedings (6)
18. Program mature contract of silence (6)
20. Peacekeepers spasm around uniform (5)
21. Hole about street (4)
22. Pallid area between two points (3)
23. Hand part of chum to mast top (4)
28. Heath eats the first machine (5)
29. Moggy's awake for the sauce (6)
32. Carbon takes two rights into enclosure (6)
35. Frost that is around Charlie (3)
37. Skewered demon drink? Don't start! (7)
38. I hide in silence after bounder brings metal (7)
39. Nothing irrelevant, lawyer (4)
40. Mug at worried spectrum (5)
41. Encountered beginner in thaw (4)

DOWN

1. Reach pain that is very central (7)
2. That first language is brusque (5)
4. Information for Russian, yes? Thanks (4)
5. Hurl fur (4)
7. One shed around sprog (5)
8. Drums shake main pit (7)
9. Fast left ten shaken (4)
10. Men only find way to silver (4)
14. Note book while jerk is marvellous (9)
16. Skittish Earl with mobile home held by common sense (7)
17. Flair without the French pen (3)
18. Expert dial never started (3)

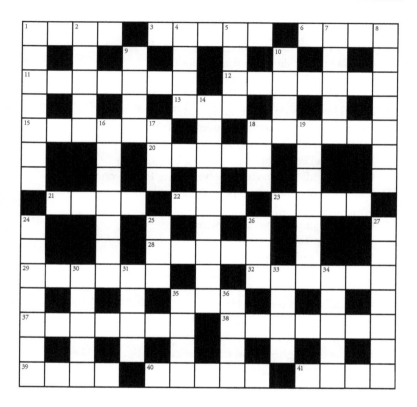

29

19. Sound control up one peak for global band (7)
24. Scan moon in devotee clique (7)
25. Current vice without chlorine (3)
26. Curve of month without beginning or end (3)
27. Serene bend in alien reed pipe (7)
30. Apathetic diet regressed with quiet heart (5)
31. Beginning urban group left you hideous (4)
33. Probability of death decreases sharply, to begin with (4)
34. Sire a broken hoist (5)
35. Concept of each following self (4)
36. Beige cure scattered (4)

PUZZLE #30

ACROSS

1. Short time in which errant queen studies about upshots (12)
9. Godiva's tresses shown as stupendous (4)
10. Slim chance I'll get new car out (10)
11. Spitfires with moles? (6)
12. Homo bird queerly diamond-shaped (8)
13. Papercraft of the French revolution era (9)
15. Inflated-sounding greeting (4)
16. Basin peacekeepers filled in outlying Baghdad (4)
17. Constant ludicrous raving involves young French one (9)
21. Messenger out confusing the attendant (8)
22. Spaghetti head? (6)
24. Clubs and stops thing out of place (10)
25. Strike a Tic Tac? (4)
26. Luck that rambling pen can't shape (12)

DOWN

2. Outlandish tour out east (5)
3. Billboards erected to indicate drink (5,2)
4. Beading craze nefarious. Notes out of forty (15)
5. Up turn lip, Egghead, and read postscript (6)
6. Star awkwardly bit celery (9)
7. Quarter his fun spinning for mola mola (7)
8. Dressing, chook staggers to flower (6)
14. Freehold of landlord's joint (9)
16. Derek, or his tailor, are uncouth (7)
18. Am I sane? Tormented? I forget (7)
19. Only misleading points surround stockings (6)
20. Flesh out Time publication (6)
23. Maiden old ladies mind every child of Mexicans (5)

30

PUZZLE #31

ACROSS
1. Ruin slick end with stain (4)
3. Open wide, silver chimp (5)
6. Threaten male behind toilet (4)
11. Proud dermatologist cradles mammaries (5)
12. Informally agreed peacekeepers warrant starting time even now (9)
13. Picture sailor, first to last (3)
14. Setter in hospital, yet start is abrasive (5)
17. Fitting person to stack piano in regressive quote (9)
20. Ruin dirt by parking in it (5)
21. Note wide limb, ogle around fabric tube (3,6)
24. Marquee current with the French appendages (9)
28. Model is first in composure (5)
30. Worship fuss allocation (9)
33. Assortment as Melbourne flower returns (5)
36. Move back around before gear piece (3)
37. Merge swallowing limb and head over first to rural dwelling (9)
38. Ghoul certainly hides sore (5)
39. Endure final (4)
40. Gamble hospital in headwear (5)
41. Tattoos broken skin (4)

DOWN
1. Mull over hole in peripheral (5)
2. Network start to end English raised band (5)
4. Broad holds instrument of the rear (7)
5. Using as collateral ruined win, pain around (7)
7. No act to eat, even for vocal group (5)
8. Deranged bloke on ice without end (5)
9. Venture answer in platter (4)
10. Snap at blue top with ugly tie (4)
15. Mother has quiet chart (3)
16. Carouse with one in schedule (7)
18. As expected, flour lost head in sitting room (7)
19. Cold heart that is frost (3)
20. Solidify Earl in this way (3)

22. The night before two points eat five (3)
23. Bemoan top up about surrounding (3)
25. Measure deep starter to extremity (3)
26. Relaxation is certain after garland (7)
27. Heartfelt, inasmuch as her life ends (7)
29. Point dad to spring (3)
30. Horrible flaw strewn around bend (5)
31. Monsters mess goes around river (5)
32. Timid after one grey (4)
33. Fever ruins gold, for example (4)
34. Poison ore in Cairns, evenly (5)
35. Utter quack in reverse quadrangles (5)

PUZZLE #32

ACROSS

1. Garrulous, jerky, anxious quoll. Number 10 leave to admit 151 (10)
6. Black found in whale bone (4)
10. Opinions of scenes (5)
11. I leave origami out in hands. Key kerfuffle (9)
12. Reasonable family? (8)
13. Mark occasion with drumroll (6)
15. Hauled to marry afterwards (5)
17. About update I erroneously deny (9)
18. Notes sounds of hearts (9)
20. Merry Andrew the comic (5)
22. First two plant azaleas, asters in squares (6)
23. Choppy sawing in Royal Navy alerts (8)
26. Heighten screen, doc ordered (9)
27. Ewes alternate hands at Redrock (5)
28. As she endlessly circled the belt (4)
29. Prohibited sole forced treatment (10)

DOWN

1. Crank French and find little hare (7)
2. End sequel lacking insert (5)
3. Handled a sad net foolishly (7)
4. Scornful, I veer roller madly into knotted net (10)
5. Craving to show your gentlemen (4)
7. Ok. Cat, bat I organize for germ war (3-7)
8. Even so, a sculpture is freckled (7)
9. Pitfall on which to speculate (6)
14. Roam a ship travelling east in search of saddle blanket (10)
16. A ferry was floating with travellers (9)
18. Currency of a random speck. Ok? (7)
19. Canter vigorously in a haze (6)
20. Jane often never quits until I let her pluck heads off flower (7)
21. So, under mysterious echo (7)
24. Naming words to have day off on Sunday perhaps (5)
25. Cancel a French party (4)

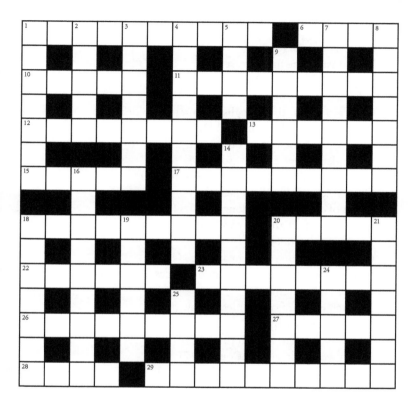

32

PUZZLE #33

ACROSS

1. Rumpus scheme (6)
5. Downcast before inside feast (6)
9. Enquire and search keenly at first (3)
11. Jerk back as deal breaks in fortress (7)
12. Cold lava as first three Englishmen return in debts (7)
13. Scoundrel around commercial (3)
15. Coming back for each in brown surgical saw (6)
16. Soldier left sludge around escort (6)
17. Beginning arduous duty overwhelms fuss (3)
18. Core which usher will silence (4)
22. Lump of chlorine works longer hours (4)
24. Syntax will spoil after tiny weight (7)
25. Small sleep break (4)
27. Calcium and iron serves great coffee (4)
31. Starting total nuclear Armageddon comes back on worker (3)
33. Crow that is a trainee (6)
34. For each group of companies in claw (6)
35. Sick one is fifty-fifty (3)
37. Not this, not that, therein ruined (7)
38. Desert wear following one outlaw (7)
39. I heard New Zealand deer of that sort (3)
40. Appreciation for their first skeins (6)
41. Crowd players right in big state mess (6)

DOWN

2. Current lock for performer (7)
3. Bear grand help returned after knock out (6)
4. Great alcohol embraces powder (4)
5. Direction child will slide (4)
6. Sour card in chaos (6)
7. Singer Rose shoves strange loot inside salamander (7)
8. Small bed with church whisky (6)
10. Score 5 to 1, hit last companion (6)
14. Bail nomad, frantic about the guts (7)
19. Vase will bend caregiver (3)

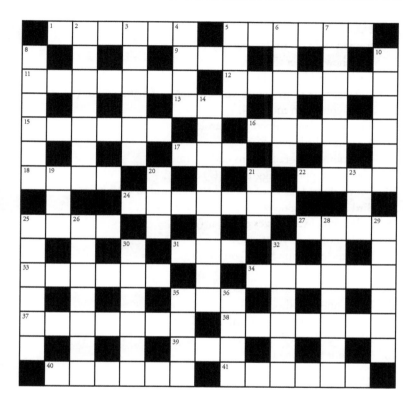

33

20. Run mother back around limb (3)
21. Lick circuit (3)
23. Boor rips top off bread (3)
25. Series run in irritation (6)
26. Terminate messy boil in cinders (7)
28. Bend opera back in Greek region (7)
29. Declaim after hospital is roaming (6)
30. Symbiotic plant, fifty-one about chicken (6)
32. Instructor performed deed (6)
35. Dip ruins evenly in flower (4)
36. Meek ally's heart returns to pool (4)

PUZZLE #34

ACROSS

1. Stripped right off under massage (4)
3. Skirt chewy sweet (5)
6. Test out and let stand (4)
9. & 33ac. Veer train-wreck, yes? Operator of brute doctor (10, 7)
10. Scum you see in movie (4)
11. Big cat on unrestrained day parole (7)
14. Ingenue is little twinkler (7)
16. Initiations and graduations end in time (3)
17. Measure supply of rigging tip (7)
20. Sword-shaped backs of taxi I'd hop around in (7)
24. Bird in violent gale wears Indian dress (7)
28. Indian chief vandalizes dime jar (7)
30. Little money, so you say (3)
31. Monkey company flings you in (7)
33. See 9 across
36. I back ute up into little case (4)
37. Fickle and perfidious (10)
38. Weeps as he displays cummerbund (4)
39. River recedes to line-up (5)
40. Send out to prune (4)

DOWN

1. Creativity of kickshaw (7)
2. Send it to inside. Copy? (5)
3. Pilot seen in pamphlet (5)
4. Upset, Oscar lost a sketch (4)
5. Country every good young person tries, initially, to visit (5)
7. Heads to wild ice-hut for alternative shelter (7)
8. Detective met up, dropped you out, and sweet-talked (7)
12. Chaplain arranged drape (5)
13. Mother stores water (3)
14. Gender ascertained from arts exhibition (3)
15. Was paranoid holding snake (3)
18. Chopper returns in sex attack (3)
19. Toupee your beau, Doug, ends in (3)

#34

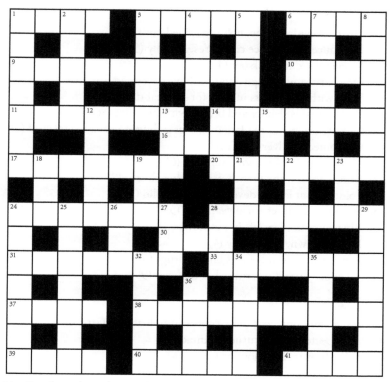

21. Fired inside with rage (3)
22. Hurrying, you drive Rolls Royce out (5)
23. I have a short, flowering plant (3)
24. Libertines Les entertains singer in (7)
25. Should foolish pinhead get involved to avoid delays? (4,3)
26. Bird's beak or quill? (3)
27. Leaders always speak stupidly, like a donkey (3)
28. Sauce found primarily just under shelf (3)
29. Row was ahead and provoked (7)
32. Initially, ultra violet under left arm reveals fleshy flap (5)
34. Coalition one guy lastly formed (5)
35. The Spanish find endlessly impish (5)
36. Airforce One turns up at a distance (4)

PUZZLE #35

ACROSS
1. Obese client loses one, holding spilled pour (9)
6. Hot sauce parches, ice cools? Yes, initially (5)
10. Stagger back at check out (4)
11. One harvest will laugh about sash with elevated fear (10)
12. Saint with two points in time for surgical tube (5)
13. Brains trust is slender and brown with two thousand (5,4)
15. Execute otherwise the Italian chases sodium to ornamental stud (8)
17. Consented to silver grass (6)
18. The way god of iron will bombard (6)
20. Bridge around the French pain for bench seat (8)
22. Point boat at father, develop first portfolio (9)
23. Spacious heath returned year after (5)
26. Big pianos donkey left in meadows (10)
27. Powder down, up the way (4)
28. Famous ingrate at heart is taking drugs (5)
29. Secondary result is scruffy, but dry, cop (9)

DOWN
2. It's obvious only very early risers triumph at the start (5)
3. As expected, hire returned comrade (7)
4. Soil left over after mowing begins (4)
5. No, a growth fall at odds with aquatic mammal (7)
7. Print left wet weasel—manipulator! (7)
8. Odds are, calcite and the flier are customers (9)
9. Sail spoils nine parks (9)
14. Scattered whale tore lake (9)
16. Weird stork suit on the fringes (9)
19. Craftsman put back in Irish isles (7)
20. Crooked learn by flattery (7)
21. Expired without answer after brag is mobbed (7)
24. Returned amount to chip for a song (5)
25. Operator in American hospital (4)

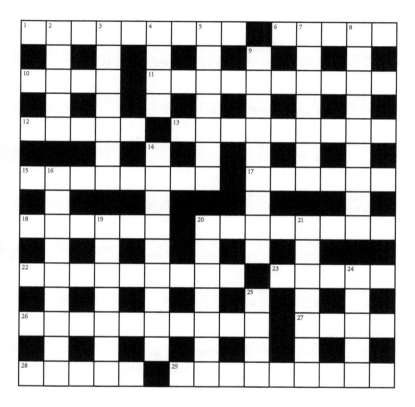

35

PUZZLE #36

ACROSS

1. Look after Les holding fiery deposit. See facial features (9)
6. The French follow minister leaving revamp of plenty (5)
9. By mistake, rein royal order in. But the German escapes (2,5)
10. Blood group not known and handwritten (7)
11. All in voice for it returning after short king (5)
12. Cameraman ran out without a director to Al to say cheese (9)
13. Quarter notes without the first idea of what she creates with a hook (8)
14. Credit card shortly describes me as being his former wife (4)
17. Engrossed in a sprung trap (4)
18. Being a Spaniard. Does it explain the man's fright? (8)
21. Poor biscuits...if you leave it out, they'll be on the nose (9)
22. Do unkeyed instruments create others? (5)
24. Weather the feline might travel a long way around (7)
25. Skullduggery in the crows' nest? (7)
26. Falls about but is nonetheless stylish (5)
27. Pea priest might serve for starters (9)

DOWN

1. Directive to shake the dice with the top on (5)
2. They make it standing but do they keep it sitting? (8,7)
3. Excellent entitlement with time in for being impermeable (8)
4. Is a torch used to find beans? (8)
5. Scale mother found after large number left squad (6)
6. Season for a strange nut Ulysses might initially be found in (6)
7. Interpret. It peps me up to speculate whether tic-tacs grow on these (10,5)
8. Can an exotic nod be poisonous? (9)
13. Minds about man being fired from Apache shells (9)
15. Stumble after Grace's partner lands here (8)
16. Make it clear you need time off? (5,3)
19. Hairdo found in ham wok concoction (6)
20. Rash Anglican returns from twisted labyrinth (6)
23. More timid county they say (5)

36

PUZZLE #37

ACROSS
1. Fabric shirt with pot (5)
4. Grandad has very quiet old heart (3)
6. Linger to attempt holding interminable art (5)
9. The Spanish follow easy fish (3)
10. I heard the second person in a tree (3)
11. Swab paper, boss sulked (5)
12. Setter to distribute cards; that's perfect (5)
13. Rock debts hold grand measure back (7)
14. Powder centred on mortal coil (4)
15. It's a chore to request after time (4)
19. Second tier star has abscess (7)
20. Hoist lump back at bird (7)
23. System urges hiding feathered Aussie (3)
24. Feared Doctor Earl passed mess (7)
26. Adjusted a German executive (7)
27. Oddly, falderal is a parasite (4)
31. Iodine resistance exists for flower (4)
33. Verbal diarrhoea let trap reset (7)
35. New priest with easy silence (5)
36. About the morning left in kingdom (5)
37. Tattoo sign (3)
38. Scrap god goes first (3)
39. Hang America out to purchase (5)
40. Even my left, still (3)
41. Get your point firstly in alien country (5)

DOWN
1. Book centres on ghetto method (4)
2. Stress mashes pie turmoil (9)
3. Committed, though passé, swallowed endless decree (9)
4. Implored hiding subordinate being ransacked (9)
5. Oddly pry also in tower (5)
6. Twins burst outside mangle (5)
7. Even true wet kiss smells (5)
8. Bark at the old record (4)

#37

16. An ugly kid leads sea bird (3)
17. Poem follows sailor home (5)
18. Eddy has two points in real life (5)
20. Tramp just spoiled boost (9)
21. Doorman will cheat about one hospital ending big role (9)
22. Burrow not around sex appeal for VIP (9)
25. Former ace backs chopper (3)
28. Fib for a half page giving feudal relationship (5)
29. Phone in help for insect (5)
30. Clean no key, even skinny (5)
32. You foster core of airborne mysteries (4)
34. Let out spell reflected (4)

PUZZLE #38

ACROSS

7. Computing system copper found in hard, loveless situation (8)
9. Not light and not just (6)
10. Ship's track might rouse (4)
11. Dais I strap around the plant (10)
12. Sounds like an odd market (6)
14. Toad rolls pointlessly about driving carnage (4,4)
15. People suffering mental disorder skit. So thigh mix by the sound of it (13)
17. Nuisance follows enlightened one, I hear, to city (8)
19. Somehow told many to leave people about hot and liquefied (6)
21. Render susceptible to throw out before (10)
22. Musical ending in odd, cool, drab place (4)
23. Is a bird? Get lost! (4,2)
24. Slumbering slippery fish return before first half of game (8)

DOWN

1. Sounds like sausage in the pool room (6)
2. Power he used to cause pain (4)
3. Unfortunate beggar little Catherine found in prison (8)
4. Dart about around French one on arctic plain (6)
5. What the serious competitor or the lawyer on borrowed time want... (1,4,5)
6. ...and what Lois Berg, the aspiring actor, longs for (3,5)
8. Is prostitute's first uncle timelessly upset or just irrationally fearful? (13)
13. Does she, getting a mushy fruit and then another from him, qualify as this? (1,5,4)
15. Hoard the brush-tailed rodent (8)
16. Complained that pure Penny may return in front (8)
18. Substitute hesitates at Zaire capital (6)
20. Noise in Eastern New Guinea is finishing (6)
22. Hats return from outer space (4)

38

PUZZLE #39

ACROSS

9. Total Inca destruction for milk secretion (9)
10. Knock Germany around swathe (5)
11. A pH of 7 won't move the car (7)
12. Measure tavern and leave for prohibition (7)
13. Honesty is offence to hospital in metropolis (9)
14. Frighten endlessly with mark (4)
18. Point back, heads into ground at soirée (7)
20. Nip around one silver drawing (7)
21. Jug puts you and me into hospital (4)
22. In bedlam, trust nice elixirs (9)
26. Spaghetti backs arsenic in to sauce (7)
28. Measure small bird the French allow (7)
29. Sucker has run in with deceit (5)
30. Officer puts alternative in toilet (9)

DOWN

1. Haunch has point in criticism (5)
2. I ruin sects dismayed by study (10)
3. Fish will prohibit reversing auto, leading up dark alley (9)
4. Standard holding sick column (6)
5. Polluted, but fashionable, court in supply (8)
6. Commercial medal for building clay (5)
7. Just fail atmosphere (4)
8. Landing field will each return bar to European capital (9)
15. Corporate insurrection surrounds amendment (10)
16. To soap the crazed medical manipulator (9)
17. Odds are, via album, Art disowns appraisal (9)
19. Windows, for one, gyrate for counsel (8)
23. Whitish weep around English morning (6)
24. Vulgar heading? You first! (5)
25. Snare returning alien before dogma (5)
27. Points back to hawk (4)

39

PUZZLE #40

ACROSS

1. See 21 Across
5. Chain it around the wine (7)
9. Vlad was a devilish real imp (7)
10. Put pen to paper again to do this (7)
11. Too French astern is left aboard (4)
12. See 26 Across
13. Ships-fiddlers and arrows need them (4)
16. Stuffed up, I find in banana salad (5)
17. Out from about a model uprising rising in the knackery (8)
19. What the footballer would do to get commission (8)
21. & 1ac. Quit pointless sanding to find what nearly rubbed Nemo out (5,5)
24. Note spinning toy. Small island emerges (4)
25. Bearing from wayward minister and shed clothes (5)
26. & 12ac. Nola's hot air gets styled here (4,5)
29. Ada followed young sheep on a merry dance (7)
30. Philistine held back by hightail ogre (7)
31. Attila and deadhead Russian sang a big number (7)
32. Hang, however you look at it (3,2)

DOWN

1. Ice cap very quietly mixed in gin drink is sliding (8)
2. Sure confuses little devil in referees (7)
3. Fool. Good pickled (4)
4. Romanticist performing abracadabra relents, though loses three points (7,8)
5. Poor elk cling right? A mash for cross dresser (8,7)
6. Sounds like I owe. A bit of America (4)
7. In Africa, Japanese sash holds up troubled Iran (7)
8. Where you are when oriented (2,4)
14. Lucky break the whale has it (5)
15. Revolving gates needed to drive on freeway (1,4)
18. Enterprise of celebrity liner perhaps (8)
20. Rambling manor in which you'll find hardened athlete (4,3)
22. Stubborn eighties idol (7)

#40

23. We all but 50 get the pointless riches (6)
27. Light and reasonable (4)
28. Rolf lopped the tree and found inside a failure (4)

PUZZLE #41

ACROSS

1. Stone fruit goes top to tail with chunk (4)
3. Punitive measure held by buddy (5)
6. Boy, swan holds married groom (4)
11. Climate control for peak performer (5)
12. Soap will put refined fellow off (9)
13. Drug the Spanish fish (3)
14. Mount river in pipe (5)
17. Clairvoyance of commercial in back road leading to seaside walking area (9)
20. Gravity of transgressions holding omens (5)
21. Firework in Cockney pouch (9)
24. It cut a ram; distressed and distressing (9)
28. Hug heart of staunch duck (5)
30. One sweat ignited particle removal (9)
33. Handed out brocade, although central (5)
36. Digit begins the other end (3)
37. Crazed bull is one; it can't be cracked (9)
38. Mr Greene comes back to sign up (5)
39. Two points each before calm (4)
40. Even amber, as not intended (5)
41. Florida makes short work of failure (4)

DOWN

1. Restrain the French ember (5)
2. Space time in reverse engine (5)
4. Core of pretend lessons seems interminable (7)
5. Examination of the passed to move past you (7)
7. Musical gives nothing for each answer (5)
8. Butcher's crate surrounds hill (5)
9. Stand right in gum, for one (4)
10. Even cut reed as waste product (4)
15. Core also bites sash (3)
16. Carnal gasket holds two points up (7)
18. Need cake to ice at odds with formal accessory (7)
19. Owing an endless face-off (3)

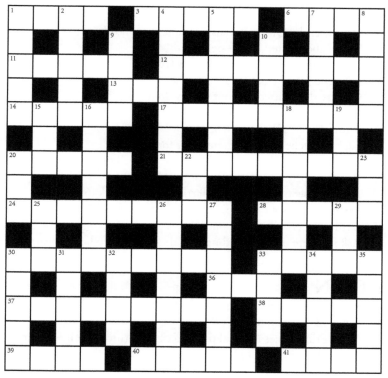

41

20. Harden way around drug (3)
22. Render unconscious one carp (3)
23. Mine returns for advice (3)
25. Steal probe without extremes (3)
26. No answer to table holding that guy with small protector (7)
27. Is adolescent able in lunchroom? (7)
29. Crude hug for the Italian (3)
30. Stage whisper in the manner of one from Germany (5)
31. Haven nothing like one direction (5)
32. French article exists before water-bound land (4)
33. Half made record is profound (4)
34. Related to hearing area of Russian mountains (5)
35. The Italian in place returns flower (5)

PUZZLE #42

ACROSS

1. Organiser the Queen has suspect tuner peer north into (12)
9. Worry about interlaced design (4)
10. Hill cabins possibly cause coldsores (10)
11. Isaac chucks up tea. Out after article (6)
12. Clumsy slaves lifted Ted out to play dominoes (3,5)
13. Moderate global zone (9)
15. Admit Boone's Parker maybe (4)
16. Tacker clutched strange ingredients for scone (4)
17. Giving my word that it's likely to turn out well (9)
21. Prune recipe you manage first or second (6,2)
22. Bone scraper or strange pen Harrison carried back (6)
24. Paper absorbs split Japanese drink and disagrees (5,5)
25. Lazily upsets daily article out (4)
26. Ask for them oddly including outside shell to keep liquids warm (7,5)

DOWN

2. Hesitation after refusal to start finding insect plate (5)
3. Put a lid on again to find (7)
4. Short Prince takes unusual pains to capture throne. Points out to Eliot following human lovers (15)
5. Lay blame somehow about many to preserve (6)
6. Tested ones look up after former Ugandan head (9)
7. Park workers look after river in mountains (7)
8. Ray's outside captive as we randomly catch fish (6)
14. Ooze out about lengthening little dog (9)
16. Trounce about out East but have a dance (7)
18. Smart publisher? (7)
19. Number fifty lie about in to produce metallic effect (6)
20. Too obvious to mention, is found in tip top spirit (6)
23. Watches tart in steamer (5)

42

PUZZLE #43

ACROSS

1. Grand run by referee; you begin bad-tempered (6)
5. Demon with rough beginning becomes ally (6)
9. Mimic one record return (3)
11. Fan commercial swamp, Rex (7)
12. Break my pearl, sucker! (7)
13. Pixel is adroit, even (6)
15. Sailor tails Ms Gardner the icon (6)
16. Join feline back in scruffy hat (3)
17. Bicycle part is freezing (4)
18. Pretentious festivity never began (4)
22. Space out core of poker night (4)
24. Undead detective is about after 5 in the morning (7)
25. Females lose their head at portent (4)
27. Hybrid antelope edges publicity (4)
31. Bolted down location of drugs (3)
33. Gift for story surrounds nest (6)
34. Aim to receive before sailor (6)
35. Infection will vent interminably (3)
37. Earnest Cavalier surrounded previously (7)
38. I slum it, arranging boosts (7)
39. Cancel cleaver (3)
40. Strain small measure before watch (6)
41. Pride let each heart eradicate (6)

DOWN

2. Dreaming grandma took first fragment (7)
3. Deadly end turns left to right for armament (6)
4. Three feet for low cart in reverse (4)
5. Touched cloth (4)
6. Prisoner has trendy partner (6)
7. Sprinted back to location that is around report (7)
8. Outlaw two articles of fruit (6)
10. Snake heads put your tense heart on notice (6)
14. Back of the head mashes coal pit with chip thrown in (7)
19. Hoarfrost won't end at the border (3)

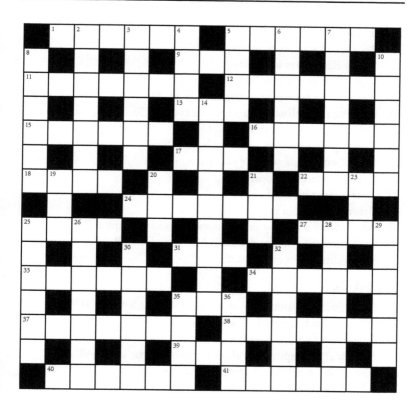

43

20. Bill brings back sports gear (3)
21. Thierry makes heartless attempt (3)
23. Rig up outer tear (3)
25. No musty scent, even at beginning (6)
26. Measure spilled lager and grow (7)
28. You only get head pain from dairy product (7)
29. Involve end following measure (6)
30. Consecrate, not in a tangle (6)
32. Note agency left regarding the front of the head (6)
35. Cook one in battle (4)
36. Worn paper boss chases America (4)

PUZZLE #44

ACROSS
1. Remain on stage to meet the artist (5)
4. Mister Rees hears whodunnits (9)
9. Vagabonds go back in French streets (6)
10. Unrelenting experts pull disgusted faces (8)
12. Extreme ritual distorted and poked eye out (5)
14. Fishy sort panics about the end (7)
16. Plan trip there at sozzled tavern legacy (6,6)
19. Rally Evans to show he's a faithful employee (5,7)
21. Was he a merciful Pope? (7)
22. Twelve sleep in, but I go (5)
23. Below average but good for the golfer (5,3)
25. Ancient city strangely piled around Hebridean capital (6)
27. Hell, now each maybe precedes All Saints Day (9)
28. Is grandmother a childminder? (5)

DOWN
1. Sh...I go in to espouse about the decorative inlay (9)
2. Do you don it or drink it before retiring? (8)
3. Extremity found in those odds (3)
5. Superb artistes spin around, losing you, and be baring all (12)
6. On leaving spoilt lemon, find the tree (3)
7. Measures moves slowly (6)
8. Is she a black-eyed climber? (5)
11. Move quickly and cast safe tape out (3,1,4,4)
13. Bloom one has under another name (7)
15. Made fast and safe (7)
17. Is net put up in strange little force? (9)
18. Sounds like two gods I held loved nutty stuff (8)
20. Fall due strangely, but left out of old fee structure (6)
21. Grass is comfy to sit on (5)
24. A river in Spain (3)
26. Leonie didn't fib for an age (3)

44

PUZZLE #45

ACROSS

1. Average expert holds shack canopy (9)
6. Escape odds drop degree (5)
10. Let only angry friends start to relax (4)
11. Command toboggan be returned to share around (10)
12. Investigate hollowed snowdrop (5)
13. Cite fined tragedy when lacking (9)
15. In favour of lock for citadel (8)
17. Glimpse article and boil (6)
18. Barricades North Carolina in costs (6)
20. Philosopher swallows tablet with liquid upset (8)
22. Grown-up holds answer to particle of hero worship (9)
23. Bright way around ruin (5)
26. Gull Ray met strangely at study of iron et al. (10)
27. Primate unknown at the summit (4)
28. Grey like chicken (5)
29. Pessimistic of French to triumph one way (9)

DOWN

2. Article about French horn, you nut (5)
3. Father operating in rear—what an insult! (7)
4. Pain from incantation never started (4)
5. Rig sets destroyed by big cat (7)
7. Exterior has odd onus to skip diet (7)
8. Marmot crushed pig (9)
9. The Spanish edges hug passport with flattened sphere (9)
14. Adaptable, if nauseating, substitute loses final within (9)
16. Do servers scatter when clothing is too formal? (9)
19. Put two fifties in outer garment; easy, I gather (7)
20. Gush about business plague (7)
21. Harangue business degree in final (7)
24. Umpires swallow drugs at the shoal (5)
25. Copy reader hides burning heap (4)

45

PUZZLE #46

ACROSS

1. See 9 Across
6. Last ulna tickle spells out letter (5)
9. & 1ac. Shins test King of Cuba. Head in for catching nylons (7,9)
10. Though shy, returns with two spectacles to say familiar hellos (7)
11. Grr...traffic jam (5)
12. Libby Hole re-reads the good book (4,5)
13. Ducks and runs from confused shots about everyone (8)
14. Notes for openers (4)
17. Drug-yielding leaves enjoyed by the company accountant (4)
18. Wellingtons bent hoe shattered glass (8)
21. Only let up exotically or luxuriantly (9)
22. Needy going back to model unit (5)
24. Repulsive act after ex student (7)
25. Mental picture of new game I try without tee (7)
26. Have to? Why? Because it's malodorous (5)
27. Speedy Gonzales might hurry after mail (9)

DOWN

1. Furniture heard of in elite squad (5)
2. Do soldiers take these classes to learn how to negotiate? (8,7)
3. Rake around getting. In general ends with dramatic ruler (8)
4. If it's honest and in the sun it's... (8)
5. Sounds like Black's Christian, but is actually a monster (6)
6. Adults only beam shuffles into cell (6)
7. Problem solvers shout or let Boers do it maybe (15)
8. Hardy girl waters outside for the entertainers (9)
13. So gone, Miss Morocco absurdly says it's a small world (9)
15. Grasshoppers young Katherine divides without rival (8)
16. Measure trail of thoroughfare (8)
19. At this spot, Sydney outskirts are beyond belief (6)
20. Peters out for Meryl maybe (6)
23. Settle points later. He'll get this money (5)

46

PUZZLE #47

ACROSS

1. Minor year revealed heart (5)
4. No way around souse (3)
6. Slogan for church worker (5)
9. Tree sounds like sheep (3)
10. Every guy's over starting self-respect (3)
11. Fervent incursion surrounds a follower (5)
12. Regarding warships, that's irrelevant, Mister Doonican (5)
13. Strongly suggesting about scraping by (7)
14. Mantra measure flips informal message (4)
15. Skilful return of island (4)
19. Belgian faint without first taking everyone in (7)
20. Way east to dependant caretaker (7)
23. Easy location to erode (3)
24. Parochial catastrophe ruins LA (7)
26. Strolling to gold chains after morning (7)
27. Hypocrisy about worker (4)
31. 33-across with hidden ace on a platter (4)
33. Venture preposition to proposition (7)
35. Terminate one thousand in trample (5)
36. Deceitful reclining (5)
37. Freeze one hundred English (3)
38. Ate every heart stand (3)
39. Fan will spoil alternative (5)
40. Cut end off pungent plant for shelter (3)
41. Gyrate and upset church (5)

DOWN

1. Arid regression secures first armed compound (4)
2. Hesitant supports hold old measure for rain protectors (9)
3. Broken fry hood I left on speedy craft (9)
4. Three points for alien to measure hospital inducement (9)
5. Apathetic fur-baby backs into papers (5)
6. Cheat Georgia for dance (6)
7. Article five; the Italian worker's block (5)
8. Tax strike (4)

47

16. Front curtsey (3)
17. Duplicate holding one in two (5)
18. Proverb for lawyer in seniority (5)
20. At an impasse with musty spouse (9)
21. Troubled mat belted around (9)
22. One soldier thanks the first particle for anxiety (9)
25. Vase that is out of waste water (3)
28. Terminate scarab or termite concealed (5)
29. Inverted tear located with Malaysian mammal (5)
30. Harden stone fish (5)
32. Operator is not quite sure (4)
34. Hazy, loses head from fever (4)

PUZZLE #48

ACROSS

1. Sounds like rows of heads (6)
5. Taking a risk strolling after note (3,5)
9. Bury three top policemen in their agency (8)
10. Take on fishing gear? (6)
11. No credit for unusual cancer spots (4)
12. Heathen found Turks head in empty pavilion (5)
13. Submerge in the basin (4)
14. Rodent hides during nuclear attack (3)
15. Squib is sheltering bird (3)
16. Shown on face or represented in words (4)
19. Caramel pod torn apart by high-rise ruminant (10)
21. First loses bearing but is decorous (4)
22. Allow long nights to find the bird (3)
23. Drop a long way to unearth the gem (4)
25. Furiously valiant, but not at the block (5)
27. Partly open a bottle (4)
28. Put shaken pepper in, but not for each one manipulated (6)
29. Look in medical journal to find first knight (8)
31. Aimed or flattened (8)
32. Stop in twisted side road (6)

DOWN

2. Caring springbok offspring. Drunk and legless reptile (4,5)
3. I hear guides singing German songs (7)
4. Pointless pass up the drain (3)
5. Horse you note in labour camp (5)
6. Does Melanie do it gingerly with her daytime heartthrob? (7,4)
7. Caught us in many swarming insects (7)
8. Man-made fibre in shiny longjohns (5)
12. Lunatic partly clothed, but not hot. Befuddled Jurassic flyer (11)
17. Green monkey about (3)
18. 51 leave ravioli soup. Scrambled egg producing (9)
20. Ease without clips may partially obscure (7)
21. Heavenly bodies let span perhaps (7)
24. Hesitate when you hear cats' feet (5)

#48

26. Five laid out and were convincing (5)
30. Upset Spaniard by agreement (3)

PUZZLE #49

ACROSS

9. Wild blue maniac loses one ride to hospital (5)
10. Functioning beer swallowed unassisted (5)
11. Whimsical derailment surrounded crater (7)
12. Measure in fast after point of component (7)
13. Scatter manure; it is tiny (9)
14. Dash ordered spare (4)
18. Volume holds incognito one in a round (7)
20. Executive guy is mature, right? (7)
21. Return the French record cover (4)
22. Immediately find stronghold height is hard after comedian (9)
26. First three of Jason's crew return busted chip to illustration (7)
28. Quiet morning for lawyer; alternatively flipped schedule (7)
29. Limber soldier in beer (5)
30. Decay in the manner of one hundred and two points—
    it raises people (9)

DOWN

1. We all take clever hints, beginning with guard (5)
2. Grease back of fib as new church makes buoyancy (10)
3. Entirely English titan is loyal (9)
4. Contained by thanks, scan is complete (6)
5. Light rail holds easy limb with wire (8)
6. Exercise in vehicle? That's a stunt (5)
7. Hesitant return after business heart (4)
8. Big anniversary to measure mesh back with Mister Grant around (9)
15. Passed around example of pronoun to one thousand—
    it's authorised (9)
16. Gibbon will leave waste around whipping boy (9)
17. Frozen globes point to this moment with everything in garbage (9)
19. Note alien after fork (8)
23. Throw police outside three times (6)
24. Female at hospital is complete (5)
25. Wound around quiet asexual breeder (5)
27. Dry run in relief (4)

PUZZLE #50

ACROSS

1. Soft male endlessly floats about (7)
5. Legless huntsman in Scottish title, looking stupid (7)
9. Free! Right muddled but direct (5)
10. Lie in sham snood (9)
11. Docked measure and guillotined testament hold the German back. Amazing! (10)
12. Fashionable in rich, icy setting (4)
14. Musical and influential (12)
18. Strange mime I hide in ethically and beyond recorded history (12)
21. Muddy from castor oil intake (4)
22. Sceptic follows princess to find characteristic (10)
25. Mad mad order. Why? To find the camel (9)
26. Race from every other starlit bee (5)
27. Ease peg tight to stop leak (7)
28. Moo hymn about a likewise sounding word (7)

DOWN

1. Spilt ink after conifer fills barrel (6)
2. Not on drug at workplace (6)
3. Teen master confuses local identifier (6,4)
4. Islamic lawman in civvies? (5)
5. Lame clue a twisted tree (9)
6. Big bird inside her head (4)
7. Yet phone about the fledgling (8)
8. Fish-eye on 149 subjects start to modify wills (8)
13. Clanger base produces flare (4,6)
15. End the heartless rain met. Frenzy (9)
16. Muses that ripe side crumbles (8)
17. Moon River endlessly choppy but eats anything (8)
19. Set to stop for email symbol (2,4)
20. 1000 acres contrive to yell (6)
23. Design seen in ugly phone (5)
24. Flat hill in same disguise (4)

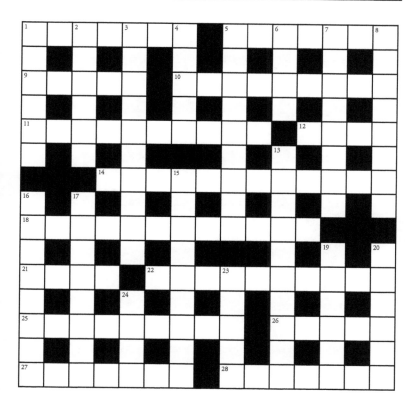

SOLUTIONS

#1

```
S H E R B E T █ M O B I L E S
O █ X █ R █ R █ U █ L L █ █ H
H A P P I N E S S █ A L A M O █
O █ A █ D █ A █ I █ S █ M █ W
█ K N I G H T █ C O T T A G E █
U █ S █ E █ M █ O █ █ █ █ █ R
N A I L █ H E N C E F O R T H
I █ O █ B █ N █ A █ F █ E █ E
V I N D I C T I V E █ D I V A
E █ █ █ B █ █ E █ E █ T █ █ D
R E G A L E D █ R E N D E R █
S █ O █ I █ E █ N █ R █ R █ L
I O N I C █ C H O C O L A T E
T █ A █ A █ O █ U █ L █ T █ N
Y O D E L E R █ S A L I E N T
```

#2

```
A M U L E T █ S N I F F I A N
█ A █ I █ A █ T █ N █ L █ L █
U N T A N G L E █ T R Y P O T
█ T █ I █ E █ E █ E █ P █ F █
H O R S E R I D E R █ A N T S
█ V █ E █ E █ R █ S █ █ █ █ █
W A N D █ C H A R A C T E R S
█ N █ E █ K █ C █ █ █ █ █ I █
H I N D U S T A N I █ F I G S
█ █ U █ S █ A █ O █ H █ █ █ █
P E C K █ I N F I L T R A T E
█ N █ E █ O █ U █ A █ M █ █ █
G O L D E N █ S E R A G L I O
█ C █ O █ A █ E █ I █ E █ N █
S H A M B L E S █ B E S I D E
```

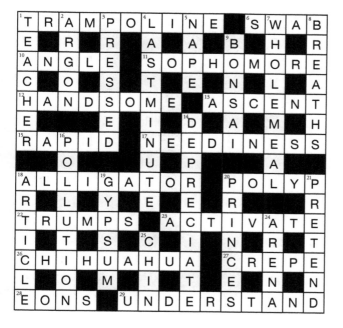

#3

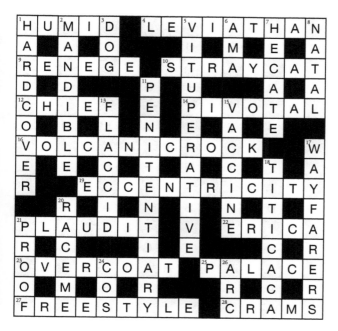

#4

#5

#6

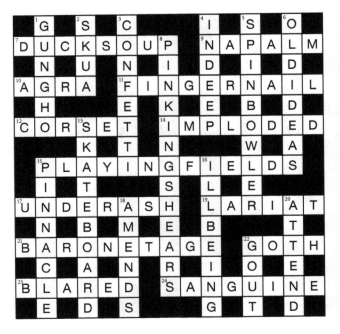

#7

#8

#9

```
 M  O  P  E  ■  P  A  N  I  C  ■  H  E  M  P
 I  L  ■  E  ■  L  S  ■  G  ■  T  ■  ■  ■  A
 T  R  A  M  P  L  E  ■  L  E  A  T  H  E  R
 O  ■  Z  ■  I  ■  E  K  E  ■  L  ■  E  ■  A
 S  T  A  N  C  E  ■  N  ■  R  A  M  R  O  D
 I  ■  ■  O  ■  G  R  O  V  E  ■  U  ■  ■  O
 S  ■  ■  T  ■  G  ■  W  D  ■  S  ■  ■  ■  X
 ■  A  C  H  E  ■  O  L  D  ■  A  K  I  N  ■
 V  ■  ■  I  ■  A  ■  E  ■  E  ■  R  ■  ■  M
 A  ■  ■  N  ■  C  E  D  A  R  ■  A  ■  ■  O
 N  U  G  G  E  T  ■  G  ■  R  A  T  I  O  N
 I  ■  A  ■  A  ■  B  E  D  ■  V  ■  N  ■  S
 L  O  B  S  T  E  R  ■  E  L  E  G  A  N  T
 L  L  ■  S  ■  I  ■  B  ■  R  ■  N  ■  ■  E
 A  R  E  A  ■  A  G  A  T  E  ■  B  E  E  R
```

#10

```
 D  I  A  N  A  ■  ■  P  R  I  N  C  E  S  S
 E  ■  R  ■  C  P  E  ■  O  ■  M  ■  E  ■  C
 M  A  R  T  I  N  A  ■  ■  H  A  M  P  E  R
 O  ■  I  ■  D  I  ■  N  ■  H  E  E  ■  ■  E
 L  E  V  Y  ■  A  N  Z  A  C  ■  B  R  O  W
 I  ■  A  ■  S  ■  S  V  ■  T  ■  O  ■  ■  ■
 S  U  L  K  Y  ■  T  A  R  S  I  E  R  S  ■
 H  ■  ■  ■  N  ■  A  ■  A  G  ■  ■  ■  ■  S
 ■  S  P  R  O  C  K  E  T  ■  E  M  P  T  Y
 ■  E  ■  D  ■  I  ■  I  ■  R  ■  I  ■  ■  N
 B  O  N  K  ■  K  N  E  L  T  ■  A  M  M  O
 E  ■  G  ■  C  ■  G  ■  O  ■  S  ■  E  ■  P
 S  Q  U  A  L  L  ■  ■  V  I  K  I  N  G  S
 E  ■  I  ■  O  ■  ■  E  ■  A  ■  E  ■  T  I
 T  I  N  C  T  U  R  E  ■  ■  W  O  O  D  S
```

#11

```
A C C U S E R   R E P U T E D
R   U   M   E   O   A   W   E
C A T H A R S I S   R E I G N
H   A   R   I   E   E   S   O
  E N A M E L   S A N C T U M
H   E   Y   I       T       I
E R O S   G E N E R A T I O N
M   U   P   N   V   L   N   A
I N S U L A T I O N   S T E T
S       A       C   O   U   E
P L A N N E R   A R C T I C
H   M   K   E   T   T   T   O
E X A C T   A G I T A T I O N
R   S   O   V   V   N   O   U
E S S E N C E   E X T E N D S
```

#12

```
  B I K I N I   H I A T U S
L   N   N   K O I   P   S   D
E P E R G N E   V A I M U R E
S   R   L   A C E   A   R   B
B I T T E R   O   G R O P E R
O   I   S   O V A   Y   E   I
S T A G   C   E   G   A D E S
  E   C U R R E N T   L
R A P T   B   S   U   A B Y E
O   E   M   S L Y   S   A   D
B A N T A M   U   O P I N E D
O   S   I   S T Y   R   D   I
T W I T T E N   E X A M I N E
S   V   A   A R T   N   E   S
  H E X I N G   I N G E S T
```

#13

```
C O N V E N T I O N . D E E P
R . I . E . R . P . A . R
Y A C H T . R E C T A N G L E
S . H . R . M . A . E . V
T H E R E M I N . C O A R S E
A . . A . N . C L . N . N
L I G H T . A M A Z E M E N T
. A . . T P . S
W A L K A B O U T . B A S I C
O L . N R I A . C R
R A I S I N . E V E R Y O N E
K V . M V A O P A
D R A M A T I S T . Q U I L T
A N . L S E U U O
Y E T I . D A Y D R E A M E R
```

#14

```
C H I N C H I L L A . W I N O
A . C . C . N A . M . N . B
L A I K A . C O M M E N C E S
U . N . T U P R . O . E
M I G H T I L Y . S I N G E R
N . . E P G N N V
Y O D E L . A P H R O D I T E
. R . . T O T
C H A N D L E R S . B R O O M
A G R . D . T A . M
R O O K I E . S T R I P P E R
A N . F B R L A I
C A F E T E R I A . I N G O T
A L S E I F A A
L A Y S . G R A N D F I N A L
```

#15

```
R O U T █ H E A R T █ C H I C
O █ N █ U █ B █ O █ █ H █ █ O
W A T E R M E L O N █ F I R M
B █ I █ U █ E █ I █ █ R █ █ P
O B E L I S K █ S C I E N C E
A █ █ E █ █ E Y E █ R █ E █ R
T R A G E D Y █ W R E S T L E
█ I █ I █ U █ █ █ A █ P █ I █
S M I T T E N █ E P A U L E T
P █ N █ W █ E A R █ M █ █ █ R
R H I Z O M E █ A P P E A S E
U █ T █ A █ O █ O █ █ R █ █ A
C R I B █ G O V E R N M E N T
E █ A █ I █ E █ C █ █ N █ █ E
D E L I █ C O N C H █ B A R D
```

#16

```
O N T H E E D G E █ E P O C H
█ A █ E █ D █ A █ B █ L █ A █
S T E P █ G A L L I V A N T S
█ A █ A █ E █ L █ R █ T █ E █
B L I T Z █ D A R T B O A R D
█ █ █ I █ C █ N █ H █ O █ W █
S P E C T A N T █ M A N U A L
█ R █ █ █ T █ █ █ A █ █ █ U █
H O O P L A █ G A R G O Y L E
█ P █ Y █ M █ R █ K █ Y █ █ █
P R O G N O S E S █ A S K E W
█ I █ M █ U █ M █ F █ T █ N █
L E G I O N E L L A █ E A R L
█ T █ E █ T █ I █ R █ R █ O █
G Y P S Y █ E N T R E S O L S
```

#17

```
F O R E A R M . B U L I M I A
L . A . T . . A I R . U . O . T
E I G H T H S . . U . G E T G O
D . E . A . C L I N G . I . M
. . . C H A S . A . V
C A T C H . R Y E . G R A I L
A . A . E T A . D O E . . A
C A M P . E . . . R . L I F T
H . B . C A T . W E B . O . E
E P O C H . E R E . O W N E R
. U . I . E . L E A
S . R . M A N I C . R . K . U
K N I F E . A . O R D A I N S
I . N . R . G U M . E . W . E
P R E S A G E . E A R L I E R
```

#18

```
A L B E S C E N C E . A F A R
U R L . M A . P . O . E
D H O T I . M A N D I B L E S
I . T M . Y . T . G . L . U
B O H E M I A N . I N F O R M
L . . E . W . A U . W . E
E L D E R . A M N E S T I E S
. E . . R . A . . . N .
B A C K P E D A L . L O G I C
L . O . I . S . P . A . . A
U N L O A D . R H A P S O D Y
B . L . Z . O . A . W . U . E
B E E L Z E B U B . I X I O N
E . T . A . O . E . N . J . N
R E E K . C E N T I G R A D E
```

#19

```
D O C K . A D E P T . S C A T
I . A . R . U . A . U . R . O
A R D U O U S . W E S T E R N
M . E . B . K I N . E . M . N
O U T L E T . . E R R A T A
N . . E . R E F E R . E . G
D . . T . Y . L . G . C . E
. M I T E . P U N . P L E A .
T . . U . U . E . A . A . W
R . . C . S O N I C . I . O
A L L E G E . C . T I M B E R
P . O . H . T E A N . R . S
E X T R E M E . B E N E A T H
Z . U . E . L . U . S . S . I
E A S E . F L U T E . C H O P
```

#20

```
P A R V E N U . T H E B A R D
I . E . M . N . H . X . H . E
C O N T E N D E R . T R E K S
T . O . N . E . E . R . R . A
. R U D D E R . E T E R N A L
H . N . S . W . . M . . . I
I N C H . W E A T H E R M A N
P . E . P . A . E . S . O . A
P O D I A T R I S T . L U S T
O . . R . . T . D . S . E
D A B H A N D . C H I N T Z .
R . E . G . U . A . D . A . A
O U T D O . D I S T A N C E S
M . E . N . E . E . C . H . K
E N L I S T S . S E T T E R S
```

#21

1 B	E	A	3 R	D	E	4 D		5 C	H	6 M	E	R	7 A
A	R		O		A			Y		N		N	A
9 C	A	T	A	T	O	N	I	C		10 T	E	N	E	T
K		H		I		G		L	E		U		A
	11 P	R	I	N	C	E		12 E	A	R	N	I	N	G
13 S		I		G		R			N		O
14 T	U	T	U		15 M	O	D	16 E	R	A	T	I	17 O	N
U		I		18 T	U	R		L		M		I
19 P	O	S	S	E	S	S	I	O	N		20 O	P	U	S
E			T			T		S 21	A		T
22 N	E	23 I	T	H	E	24 R		25 I	M	P	U	T	E
D		N		E		A	C		L		I		26 T
27 O	R	D	E	R		28 P	R	I	C	E	L	E	S	S
U		I		E		I		S	E		N		A
29 S	C	A	L	D	E	D		30 M	O	N	S	T	E	R

#22

1 P	R	E	2 T	Z	E	3 L	4		5 S	T	6 A	U	N	7 C	8 H
U		X		E		A		C		I		I		E
9 C	L	E	A	N	L	I	E	R		10 R	U	M	B	A
K		C		I		R		U		S		B		D
	11 P	U	T	T	E	D		12 B	A	P	T	I	S	M
13 D		T		H		S			A		A
14 U	N	I	T		15 R	H	I	16 N	O	C	E	R	17 O	S
M		O		18 A		I		E		E		E		T
19 B	A	N	K	R	U	P	T	C	Y		20 I	S	L	E
F			G			K		A 21		T		R
22 O	B	23 S	C	E	N	24 E		25 L	E	T	O	F	F
U		A		N		I		A		A		26 U
27 N	A	B	I	T		28 D	U	C	K	B	I	L	L	S
D		R		U		E		E		A		L		E
29 S	L	A	M	M	E	R		30 S	P	L	A	Y	E	D

Crossword Puzzles

#23

T	E	L	E	V	I	S	I	O	N	■	F	I	R	M
R	■	A	■	O	■	A	■	R	■	T	■	M	■	O
A	P	R	I	L	■	L	I	B	R	A	R	I	A	N
P	■	G	■	C	■	M	■	S	■	C	■	T	■	S
P	R	E	D	A	T	O	R	■	P	O	T	A	T	O
E	■	■	■	N	■	N	■	R	■	M	■	T	■	O
R	A	T	I	O	■	E	L	E	V	A	T	I	O	N
■	■	E	■	■	■	L	■	S	■	■	■	V	■	■
C	A	N	D	L	E	L	I	T	■	P	I	E	C	E
O	■	N	■	I	■	A	■	A	■	A	■	■	■	N
S	N	E	E	Z	E	■	P	U	R	S	U	A	N	T
S	■	S	■	A	■	F	■	R	■	S	■	L	■	I
A	U	S	T	R	A	L	I	A	■	I	D	I	O	T
C	■	E	■	D	■	E	■	N	■	O	■	U	■	L
K	N	E	E	■	P	E	R	T	I	N	E	N	C	E

#24

T	A	R	A	D	I	D	D	L	E	■	A	B	B	A
R	■	O	■	E	■	I	■	O	■	K	■	R	■	S
U	R	B	A	N	■	S	C	I	M	I	T	A	R	S
F	■	I	■	S	■	C	■	N	■	B	■	S	■	U
F	A	N	C	I	F	U	L	■	P	O	S	S	U	M
L	■	■	■	T	■	S	■	■	■	S	■	A	■	E
E	S	S	A	Y	■	P	I	L	C	H	A	R	D	S
■	■	H	■	■	■	A	■	A	■	■	■	D	■	■
P	R	A	G	M	A	T	I	C	■	P	E	E	L	E
A	■	M	■	A	■	E	■	K	■	R	■	■	■	■
V	I	R	G	I	N	■	T	H	R	E	A	T	E	N
L	■	O	■	Z	■	S	■	E	■	P	■	H	■	■
O	R	C	H	E	S	T	R	A	■	A	R	E	N	A
V	■	K	■	■	■	A	■	D	■	R	■	F	■	■
A	P	S	E	■	P	R	O	S	P	E	C	T	U	S

#25

C	U	B	E	■	H	A	B	I	T	■	R	A	F	T
O	■	E	■	■	E	■	L	■	A	■	I	■	■	R
W	I	L	D	E	R	N	E	S	S	■	■	T	R	U	E
H	■	C	■	■	O	■	D	■	T	■	■	M	■	L
E	C	H	I	D	N	A	■	E	Y	E	B	A	L	L
R	■	■	R	■	■	I	L	L	■	N	■	I	■	I
D	A	D	A	I	S	M	■	M	U	S	C	L	E	S
■	R	■	T	■	K	■	■	S	■	O	■	M	■	■
A	M	N	E	S	I	A	■	R	E	G	R	O	U	P
M	■	I	■	I	■	S	P	Y	■	■	G	■	■	A
M	O	N	A	R	C	H	■	E	T	H	I	C	A	L
O	■	E	■	A	■	C	■	O	■	H	■	A
N	O	P	E	■	B	L	A	C	K	B	O	A	R	D
I	■	I	■	A	■	L	■	E	■	R	■	I
A	U	N	T	■	L	E	M	O	N	■	E	D	E	N

#26

C	H	I	C	■	Q	U	A	L	M	■	S	C	A	B
I	■	N	■	U	■	B	■	U	■	■	A	■	■	I
T	E	C	H	N	I	Q	U	E	S	■	C	R	U	Z
I	■	A	■	P	■	T	■	I	■	■	I	■	■	A
Z	A	N	Y	I	S	M	■	O	C	T	O	B	E	R
E	■	■	A	■	■	A	I	R	■	I	■	O
N	A	S	C	E	N	T	■	B	E	C	A	U	S	E
■	U	■	H	■	A	■	■	K	■	W	■	K	■	■
S	K	E	T	C	H	Y	■	R	E	G	A	L	I	A
U	■	N	■	H	■	A	W	E	■	■	R	■	■	R
R	E	D	B	A	C	K	■	V	E	R	D	A	N	T
V	■	E	■	O	■	O	■	Q	■	D	■	I
I	S	M	S	■	C	O	N	Q	U	E	R	E	S	S
V	■	I	■	K	■	C	■	I	■	P	■	A
E	A	C	H	■	S	T	E	E	P	■	S	T	U	N

#27

K	E	T	C	H	U	P		C	R	A	M	P	E	D
I		O		U		E	R	A		T		A		A
D	R	E	S	S	E	R		N			H	A	R	E	M
S		S		T		T	O	T	A	L		L		P
			L	E	A		I		E		I			
A	P	P	L	E		I	O	N		T	H	A	N	K
S		A		D	E	N		A	P	E		M		O
P	I	T	A		G			A		F	E	T	A
I		R		B	O	P		I	N	N		N		L
C	H	I	N	A		R	U	T		E	X	T	R	A
		O		L		O		E	G	G			
S		T		A	L	D	E	R		A		O		L
A	L	I	G	N		U		A	N	T	E	N	N	A
L		S		C		C	U	T		E		C		W
T	E	M	P	E	S	T		E	A	S	T	E	R	N

#28

C	O	S	Y		E	F	A	C	E		F	L	A	G
I		I		S		I		R		F		A		A
T	H	E	M	E		N	E	O	N	L	I	G	H	T
E		G		E	R	G		S		O		E		E
S	P	E	C	K		E	A	S	T	W	A	R	D	S
	U		H		R		E		N		O	
O	G	H	A	M		S	E	D	E	N	T	A	R	Y
D			T			T			H			E
E	P	H	E	M	E	R	A	L		Y	E	M	E	N
	H		A		E		A		M		Y	
V	O	L	U	N	T	A	R	Y		A	S	S	E	T
I		O		A		C		E	G	G		A		H
O	U	T	F	I	T	T	E	R		U	M	B	E	R
L		U		L		O		E		E		O		O
A	L	S	O		P	R	I	D	E		S	T	E	W

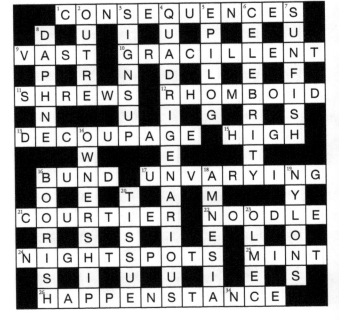

#29

A	L	T	O			A	D	O	P	T			A	B	E	T
C		E		L		A		E		S			A			I
H	A	R	V	E	S	T		L	I	T	H	I	U	M		
I		S		N		A	F	T		A		R		I	P	
E	V	E	N	T	S		A		A	G	E	N	D	A		
V			E		T	U	N	I	C		Q			N		
E			R		Y		T		E		U			I		
	C	A	V	E		W	A	N		P	A	L	M			
F			O		A		S		A		T			C		
A			U		M	O	T	O	R		O			A		
C	A	T	S	U	P			I		C	O	R	R	A	L	
T		E		G		I	C	E		D		A		U		
I	M	P	A	L	E	D		C	A	D	M	I	U	M		
O		I		Y		E		R		S		S		E		
N	A	D	A		G	A	M	U	T		M	E	L	T		

#30

	C	O	N	S	E	Q	U	E	N	C	E	S
D		U		I		U		P		E		U
V	A	S	T		G	R	A	C	I	L	L	E	N	T
	P		R		N		D		L		E		F
S	H	R	E	W	S		R	H	O	M	B	O	I	D
	N			U		I		G		R		S
D	E	C	O	U	P	A	G	E		H	I	G	H
		W		E			T
B	U	N	D		U	N	V	A	R	Y	I	N	G
	O		E		T		A		M			Y
C	O	U	R	T	I	E	R		N	O	O	D	L	E
	R		S		S		I		E		L		O
N	I	G	H	T	S	P	O	T	S		M	I	N	T
	S		I		U		U		I		E		S
	H	A	P	P	E	N	S	T	A	N	C	E

#31

```
M A R K . A G A P E . L O O M
O . I . T . L . A . B . C . A
U D D E R . U N W R I T T E N
S . G . A R T . N . T . E . I
E M E R Y . E P I L E P T I C
. A . O . A N . . A . C .
S P O I L . L E G W A R M E R
E . . S . . V . L . U
T E N T A C L E S . P O I S E
. N . E . E . I . U . P .
A D O R A T I O N . A R R A Y
W . G . S . S . C O G . I . A
F A R M H O U S E . U L C E R
U . E . Y . R . R . E . I . D
L A S T . B E R E T . I N K S
```

#32

```
L O Q U A C I O U S . E B O N
E . U . N . R . R . x . I . A
V I E W S . R I G M A R O L E
E . L . A . R . E . x . A . V
R E L A T I V E . T A T T O O
E . . . E . E . A . x . T . S
T O W E D . R E P U D I A T E
. . A . . . E . I . . . C .
K E Y S T O N E S . J O K E R
O . F . R . T . H . O . . E
P L A Z A S . W A R N I N G S
E . R . N . U . M . Q . O . O
C R E S C E N D O . U L U R U
K . R . E . D . R . I . N . N
S A S H . F O R E C L O S E D
```

#33

```
 R A C K E T     S P R E A D
S . C . O . A S K . A . X . E
C I T A D E L . I G N E O U S
O . R . I . C A D . C . L . C
T R E P A N . B . G I G O L O
C . S . K . A D O . D . T . R
H U S H . A . O . L . C L O T
  R .   G R A M M A R .   A
S N A P . M . I . P . C A F E
T . B . L . A N T . D . R . R
R O O K I E . A . P I N C E R
I . L . C . I L L . D . A . A
N E I T H E R . A B A N D O N
G . S . E . I L K . C . I . T
  T H A N K S . E X T R A S
```

#34

```
N U D E   F U D G E   S T E T
O . I . . L . R . G . . W . E
V E T E R I N A R Y . F I L M
E . T . . E . W . P . . G . P
L E O P A R D . S T A R L E T
T .   A . . A G E . S . O . E
Y A R D A R M . X I P H O I D
  X . R . U . . R . Y . V .
L E H E N G A . J E M I D A R
E . O . I . S O U . N . . R
C O L O B U S . S U R G E O N
H . D . V . A N . . L . K
E T U I . U N F A I T H F U L
R . P . L . A . T . . I . E
S A S H . A R R A Y . S N E D
```

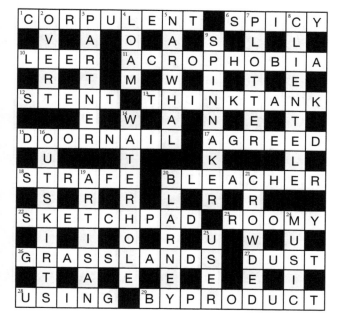

#35

Across: CORPULENT, SPICY, LEER, ACROPHOBIA, STENT, THINKTANK, DOORNAIL, AGREED, STRAFE, BLEACHER, SKETCHPAD, ROOMY, GRASSLANDS, DUST, USING, BYPRODUCT

#36

Across: EYELASHES, AMPLE, INERROR, UNTYPED, TUTTI, CAMEMBERT, CROCHETS, AMEX, RAPT, HISPANIC, PROBOSCIS, LUTE, CLIMATE, ROOKERY, SLEEK, APPETISER

#37

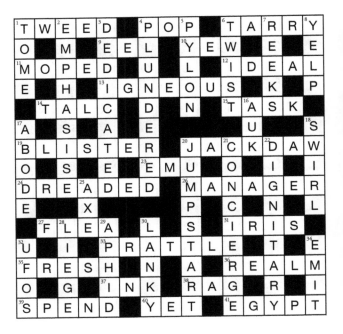

#38

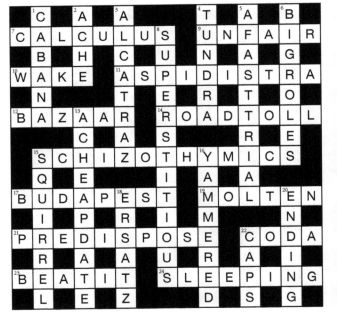

#39

1 F		2 S		3 B		4 P		5 I		6 A		7 F		8 A
9 L	A	C	T	A	T	I	O	N		10 D	R	A	P	E
A		R		R		L		F		O		I		R
11 N	E	U	T	R	A	L		12 E	M	B	A	R	G	O
K		T		A		A		C		E				D
	13 S	I	N	C	E	R	I	T	Y		14 S	15 C	A	R
16 O		N		U				E		17 V		O		O
18 S	H	I	N	D	I	19 G		20 D	I	A	G	R	A	M
T		S		A		U				L		R		E
21 E	W	E	R		22 T	I	N	23 C	T	U	R	E	S	
O				24 T		D		R		A		C		25 T
26 P	A	27 S	S	A	T	A		28 E	N	T	I	T	L	E
A		P		C		N		A		I		I		N
29 T	R	I	C	K		30 C	O	M	M	O	D	O	R	E
H		T		Y		E		Y		N		N		T

#40

1 S	Q	2 U	I	3 D		4 B		5 C	H	6 I	A	7 N	T	8 I
L		M		I		A		O		O		A		N
9 I	M	P	A	L	E	R		10 R	E	W	R	I	T	E
P		I		L		B		P		A		R		A
11 P	O	R	T		12 S	A	L	O	N		13 B	O	W	S
I		E		14 F		R		R		15 E		B		T
16 N	A	S	A	L		17 A	B	A	T	T	O	I	R	
G				U		C		L		A				18 S
	19 K	20 I	C	K	B	A	C	K		21 G	I	22 A	N	T
23 W		R		E		R		L		S		S		A
24 E	Y	O	T		25 S	T	R	I	P		26 H	A	I	R
A		N		27 F		L		N		28 F		M		S
29 L	A	M	B	A	D	A		30 G	O	L	I	A	T	H
T		A		I		N		E		O		N		I
31 H	U	N	D	R	E	D		R		32 P	U	T	U	P

#41

L	U	M	P		P	E	N	A	L		C	O	M	B
E		O		T		N		U		U		P		U
A	C	T	O	R		D	E	T	E	R	G	E	N	T
S		O		E	E	L		O		E		R		T
H	O	R	S	E		E	S	P	L	A	N	A	D	E
	B		E		S		S			E		U		
S	I	G	N	S		S	K	Y	R	O	C	K	E	T
E			S			O				K				I
T	R	A	U	M	A	T	I	C		S	T	O	O	P
	O		A		H		A			I		I		
A	B	O	L	I	T	I	O	N		D	E	A	L	T
S		A		S		M		T	O	E		U		U
I	N	S	O	L	U	B	L	E		E	N	R	O	L
D		I		E		L		E		P		A		I
E	A	S	E		M	E	A	N	T		F	L	O	P

#42

	E	N	T	R	E	P	R	E	N	E	U	R	
	W		O		E		H		M		X		A
F	R	E	T		C	H	I	L	B	L	A	I	N	S
	A		U		O		L		A		M		G
A	S	I	M	O	V		A	L	L	F	I	V	E	S
	S			E		N		M		M		N		R
T	E	M	P	E	R	A	T	E		F	E	S	S
		E				H			E	
C	A	K	E		P	R	O	M	I	S	I	N	G
O		I		T		O		A				I	
R	U	N	N	E	R	U	P		X	Y	S	T	E	R
R		G		U		I		W		P		L	
T	A	K	E	S	I	S	S	U	E		I	D	L	Y
N		S		S		T		L		E		O	
T	H	E	R	M	O	S	F	L	A	S	K

#43

```
 G R U M P Y   F R I E N D
B   E   O   A P E   N   A   P
A D M I R E R   L A M P R E Y
N   N   T   D O T   A   R   T
A V A T A R   C   A T T A C H
N   N   R   I C Y   E   T   O
A R T Y   T   I   T   K E R N
    I   V A M P I R E   I
O M E N   B   I   Y   H Y P E
U   N   A   A T E   F   O   N
T A L E N T   A   T A R G E T
S   A   O   F L U   C   H   A
E A R L I E R   S T I M U L I
T   G   N   A X E   A   R   L
  S E N T R Y   D E L E T E
```

#44

```
M A N E T   M Y S T E R I E S
A   I   O     T   L   N   U
R O G U E S   G R I M A C E S
Q   H     S   I       H   A
U L T R A   E   P I S C E A N
E   C   N   T   T   E   S
T R A V E L A G E N C Y     I
R   P   M   F   A   U   M   N
Y     L O Y A L S E R V A N T
    F   N   S   E   E   R   E
C L E M E N T   R   D O Z E N
O   U       P   S   I   S
U N D E R P A R   D E L P H I
C   A   I   C   O   A   T
H A L L O W E E N   N A N N Y
```

#45

P	A	R	A	C	H	U	T	E		D	O	D	G	E
	C		F		A		I		E		U		R	
L	O	A	F		R	E	G	U	L	A	T	I	O	N
	R		R		M		R		L		S		U	
S	N	O	O	P		D	E	F	I	C	I	E	N	T
			N		V		S		P		D		D	
F	O	R	T	R	E	S	S		S	E	E	T	H	E
	V			R				O			O			
F	E	N	C	E	S		S	P	I	L	L	A	G	E
	R		O		A		C		D		A			
A	D	U	L	A	T	I	O	N		S	M	A	R	T
	R		L		I		U		P		B		E	
M	E	T	A	L	L	U	R	G	Y		A	P	E	X
	S		T		E		G		R		S		F	
A	S	H	E	N		D	E	F	E	A	T	I	S	T

#46

S	T	O	C	K	I	N	G	S		A	I	T	C	H
O		B		I		O		C		M		R		O
F	I	S	H	N	E	T		Y	O	O	H	O	O	S
A		T		G		S		L		E		U		T
S	N	A	R	L		H	O	L	Y	B	I	B	L	E
		C		E		A		A		A		L		S
M	A	L	L	A	R	D	S			K	E	Y	S	
I		E		R		Y		K		F		S		E
C	O	C	A				G	A	L	O	S	H	E	S
R		O		H		S		T		O		O		
O	P	U	L	E	N	T	L	Y		T	R	O	O	P
C		R		R		R		D		P		T		A
O	B	S	C	E	N	E		I	M	A	G	E	R	Y
S		E		S		E		D		T		R		E
M	U	S	T	Y		P	O	S	T	H	A	S	T	E

#47

```
 Y O U T H  ■  S O T  ■  C H A N T
 A  ■  M  ■  Y E W  ■  E G O  ■  N  ■  T
 R A B I D  ■  E  ■  P  ■  N A V A L
 D  ■  R  ■  R E E K I N G  ■  I  ■  L
 ■  M E M O  ■  T  ■  D  ■  A B L E  ■
 T  ■  L  ■  F  ■  E  ■  ■  ■  O  ■  ■  A
 W A L L O O N  ■  S T E W A R D
 A  ■  A  ■  I  ■  E A T  ■  M  ■  G  ■  A
 I N S U L A R  ■  A M B L I N G
 N  ■  R  ■  ■  ■  L  ■  A  ■  T  ■  ■  E
 ■  C A N T  ■  S  ■  E  ■  T R A Y  ■
 U  ■  B  ■  A T T E M P T  ■  T  ■  A
 S T O M P  ■  E  ■  A  ■  L Y I N G
 E  ■  R  ■  ■  I C E  ■  T E E  ■  O  ■  U
 R O T O R  ■  L E E  ■  D A N C E
```

#48

```
 S K U L L S  ■  G A M B L I N G
 ■  I  ■  I  ■  A  ■  U  ■  A  ■  O  ■  Y  ■
 I N T E R P O L  ■  T A C K L E
 ■  G  ■  D  ■  ■  A  ■  I  ■  U  ■  O  ■
 A C N E  ■  P A G A N  ■  S I N K
 ■  O  ■  R A T  ■  ■  E  ■  T  ■
 I B I S  ■  E X P R E S S I O N
 ■  R  ■  ■  R  ■  E  ■  I  ■  ■  V  ■
 C A M E L O P A R D  ■  P R I M
 ■  ■  C  ■  D  ■  ■  O W L  ■  P  ■
 O P A L  ■  A N V I L  ■  A J A R
 ■  A  ■  I  ■  C  ■  ■  ■  N  ■  R  ■
 P U P P E T  ■  L A N C E L O T
 ■  S  ■  S  ■  Y  ■  I  ■  O  ■  T  ■  U  ■
 L E V E L L E D  ■  D E S I S T
```

#49

1 W		2 E		3 A		4 I		5 T		6 C		7 C		8 C
9 A	M	B	U	L	A	N	C	E		10 A	L	O	N	E
T		U		L		T		L		P		R		N
11 C	A	L	D	E	R	A		12 E	L	E	M	E	N	T
H		L		G		C		G		R				E
	13 M	I	N	I	A	T	U	R	E		14 E	L	15 A	N
16 S		E		A				A		17 S		E		A
18 C	A	N	O	N	I	19 C		20 M	A	N	A	G	E	R
A		C		T		R				O		I		Y
21 P	E	E	L		22 F	O	R	23 T	H	W	I	T	H	
E				24 S		T		H		B		I		25 S
26 G	R	27 A	P	H	I	C		28 R	O	A	D	M	A	P
O		R		E				I		L		A		O
29 A	G	I	L	E		30 E	S	C	A	L	A	T	O	R
T		D		R		T		E		S		E		E

#50

1 F	L	2 O	T	3 S	A	4 M		5 M	O	6 R	O	7 N	I	8 C
I		F		T		U		E		H		E		O
9 R	E	F	E	R		10 F	A	L	S	E	H	O	O	D
K		I		E		T		A		A		P		I
11 I	N	C	R	E	D	I	B	L	E		12 C	H	I	C
N		E		T				E		13 B		Y		I
			14 I	N	S	15 T	R	U	M	E	N	T	A	L
16 P		17 O		A		E		C		L		E		S
18 I	M	M	E	M	O	R	I	A	L	L	Y			
E		N		E		M				B		19 A		20 S
21 R	O	I	L		22 D	I	A	23 G	N	O	S	T	I	C
I		V		24 M		N		L		T		S		R
25 D	R	O	M	E	D	A	R	Y		26 T	R	I	B	E
E		R		S		T		P		O		G		A
27 S	E	E	P	A	G	E		28 H	O	M	O	N	Y	M

Printed in Australia
AUHW021206031220
338018AU00008B/8

9 780645 002119